# IMPOSSIBLY PREGNANT

## Nicola Marsh

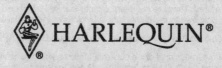

TORONTO • NEW YORK • LONDON
AMSTERDAM • PARIS • SYDNEY • HAMBURG
STOCKHOLM • ATHENS • TOKYO • MILAN • MADRID
PRAGUE • WARSAW • BUDAPEST • AUCKLAND

For Heath, my littlest hero and very own precious miracle

ISBN 0-373-03866-6

IMPOSSIBLY PREGNANT

First North American Publication 2005.

Copyright © 2005 by Nicola Marsh.

# CHAPTER ONE

*'There is no such thing as the perfect man.'*
                              *Keely Rhodes, age 19.*

'MBA. Nine o'clock!'

Keely Rhodes didn't waste time answering her friend and co-worker, Emma Radfield. Instead, she slowly turned her head ninety degrees to the left, trying to look nonchalant as she checked out the Major Babe Alert.

However, rather than your average, run-of-the-mill babe, who occasionally popped into the sleek offices of Melbourne's premier corporate website agency, WWW Designs, in search of the very best in Internet technology, this guy turned out to be the last person she had expected to see.

'What do you think?' Emma muttered under her breath, far less subtle in her attempt to ogle the guy as she craned her neck and elbowed Keely in the ribs.

*I think I've died and gone to heaven,* Keely thought, eyeing every glorious inch of the six-foot-three, broad-shouldered frame as he strode towards the reception desk.

Lachlan Brant was one fine specimen—and, by the confident charisma he oozed on the radio, probably knew it too.

'That good, huh?'

Tearing her gaze away from him, Keely fixed her friend with a curious stare. 'Don't you recognise him?'

Emma shook her head. 'Uh-uh. Believe me, if I'd seen that dreamboat before I would've remembered.'

'The name Lachlan Brant ring any bells?'

'*The* Lachlan Brant?' Emma scanned him from head to foot and dabbed at the corner of her mouth. 'Wow, he's got the bod to match that incredibly sexy voice. Excuse me while I drool.'

'Yeah, he's not bad.'

As her friend quirked an eyebrow, Keely grinned. 'Okay, he's pretty cute.'

Emma's other eyebrow joined the first.

'Make that good-looking.'

If Emma's eyebrows shot any higher they would be hidden under her blonde fringe.

Keely held up her hands in surrender. 'Okay, he's hot. Hotter than hot. He's so hot he's burning up. There, satisfied?'

Her friend sighed. 'I would be if a guy like that looked twice at me.'

Keely rolled her eyes. 'Yeah, right. Like you're interested in anyone but Harry Buchanan. Though for the life of me I can't understand why you're still pining over your first love. Get over it already.'

At the mention of Harry, Emma's eyes glazed over as if lost in some precious private memory.

Keely made an exasperated sound akin to a snort. 'Anyone ever tell you you're a hopeless romantic?'

Emma smiled. 'And I wouldn't have it any other way. What do you think he's doing here?'

Filling her cup from the water-cooler and taking several long gulps to dislodge the lump of foreboding in her throat, Keely hoped to God it wasn't for the reason she suspected.

'Who knows? He's probably dating our illustrious leader.'

Or else he'd discovered the real identity of the caller who had given him more than he'd bargained for last week on his popular radio talkback show.

'No way! He'd have better taste than that, surely?'

Keely shrugged, not in the mood to dish the dirt on Rabid Raquel, the boss from hell, as most of her employees liked to call her. Right now, she was torn between wanting to keep an eye on Lachlan Brant and running back to her office and hiding from him.

Besides, she had more important things to think about, like putting the finishing touches to the website for Melbourne's largest athletic company, designing an upbeat site for *Flirt*, the newest women's magazine about to hit the shelves, and planning Emma's surprise birthday party.

'I need to get back to work,' she said, casting one final appreciative glance in Lachlan Brant's direction before turning away.

Emma sighed. 'Yeah, me too. Lunch at Sammy's? Midday? I'll e-mail Tahlia.'

'If she can tear herself away. Our Director of Sales seems tied to her desk these days.'

'She's gunning for that promotion, you know.'

Keely nodded. If anyone understood, she should. After all, wasn't that one of the main driving forces behind her maniacal hours at the moment? She'd coveted the role of Director of Graphic Design for the last year and might have a shot at the job if Nadia would ever announce her pregnancy.

'Fine, but if she misses one more of our lunches she'll become a very dull girl. You know what they say, all work and no play…'

Emma sent her a sceptical look.

Keely chuckled. 'You're right. As if anything about Tahlia could ever be dull.'

Tahlia Moran was brash, effervescent and the life and soul of every party. Throw in gorgeous and confident and it was little wonder that Keely felt like faded wallpaper next to her other closest friend.

'See you at midday.'

However, before Keely could make her escape, Chrystal, receptionist extraordinaire—and all-round good-time gal if the office rumour mills were correct—waved her over.

Thankful she'd worn her favourite power suit today, Keely strolled across the chrome and glass foyer as if facing Lachlan Brant, her would-be nemesis, was something she did every day.

'Keely, Ms Wilson wants to see you in her office for a second before you pop back here and take Mr

Brant up.' Chrystal flashed her an Oh-goody-look-what-Santa-brought-me-this-year smile as she stared up at Lachlan Brant—her next apparent intended victim in the bedroom stakes—with adoration, barely casting Keely a second glance.

Trying to keep her nerves at bay and wondering what Raquel wanted—and why *she* had to show him up to the boss's office—Keely schooled her face into what she hoped was a professional mask and turned to face him.

'Hi, I'm Keely Rhodes. If you'd like to take a seat, I'll be with you shortly.'

Then it happened.

The man she'd publicly berated on radio turned and fixed her with a penetrating stare, the deep blue of his eyes highlighted by a shirt of the same colour.

And her heart lurched.

For the first time in her twenty-six years, the organ she'd managed to shield from breaking by only dating Mr Averages did some weird pumping that sent blood pounding through her body at a million beats a minute.

'Pleased to meet you.' He smiled and held out his hand—her heart didn't stand a chance.

Keely didn't believe in love at first sight. She was a realist who had both feet firmly planted on the ground and it hadn't steered her wrong to date. Why have romantic notions like Emma or follow nebulous predictions like Tahlia? Wishing for something that would never come true was asking for heartache and she had no intention of taking a fall.

Aware that she'd hesitated a fraction too long, Keely quickly slid her hand into his and shook it, the warmth of his touch doing strange things to her insides as his long, tapered fingers closed over hers.

Now she knew for sure. Not only had her heart flipped out, her common sense had joined the party. Since when did a mere handshake feel like an intimate touch designed for her and her alone?

'I'll be waiting.' His deep voice washed over her, so much richer, mellower, in person than over the airwaves.

How many nights had she lain awake listening to this man and the advice he dished out to the masses, listening to his voice for the sheer pleasure of it? She'd imagined an older man, someone with a wealth of life experience, till she'd seen his photo in the newspaper, though Lachlan Brant in grainy print was nothing compared to the man in the flesh.

Mentally shaking herself out of her reverie, she extracted her hand and tried to get a grip—on her wits, not the man looking at her with an amused gleam in those all-knowing eyes.

'Fine. I'll be back soon,' she said, wondering what it was about him that had her so flustered.

So he had a great body, a soulful voice and a lethal smile. That didn't make him God's gift to women. Or did it?

He also had a degree in psychology and analysed

people for a living, a fact she'd rubbed his nose in during her five-minute brush with fame—or infamy—last week. And boy, would she be in trouble if he recognised her as the crackpot who had made scathing fun of him during that call. 'Quack', 'thick as a brick', and 'out of touch' were a few of the insults she'd levelled at him that sprang to mind—and they'd been the tame ones!

Hoping her legs wouldn't wobble, she walked away, resisting the urge to glance over her shoulder and see if he was checking her out.

*As if.* Since when did guys like him go for girls like her? Though she'd conquered her eating disorder years ago, she hadn't shed her inhibitions regarding her body along with the excess kilos. Though she looked okay, she wasn't a patch on the waif look that most men favoured these days—and never would be.

Reaching Raquel's door, she cast aside her body-image issues, took a deep breath and entered after knocking twice.

'About time you got here. What took you so long?'

Though Raquel Wilson was a competent leader, with enough drive to take WWW Designs into the next decade, her people skills were on a par with those of an angry Rottweiler. In fact, several employees had taken to calling her Raquel the Rottie behind her back, and Lord help them if she ever found out. Keely had a sneaking suspicion that in this case the Rottie's bite would be every bit as bad as her bark.

Keely gritted her teeth and fixed a smile on her face. 'I was waylaid by a client.'

'Lachlan Brant, you mean?' Raquel's eyes took on a predatory gleam, the same look she got whenever a lucrative client set foot in the office.

'Uh-huh.'

'Good.' Raquel threw the pen she'd been holding on top of a pile of paperwork that looked as if it would keep her chained to her desk for the next decade. 'He's your new assignment.'

*Oh-oh.* When Raquel said 'assignment', it meant trouble. Co-workers avoided one of her special assignments like the plague—she demanded you tail the client like a detective, finding out every nitty-gritty detail to make sure their account was the best and therefore would lure further big business for the company. In a way, that was what kept WWW Designs at the top. However, the thought of wearing the gorgeous Lachlan Brant like a second skin for any length of time had Keely wanting to hotfoot it to the nearest ice cream parlour—and she'd kicked that habit a long time ago.

Resisting the urge to run as fast as her legs could carry her, Keely did her best to look keen. 'Sounds like a wonderful opportunity but I'm kind of snowed under with other accounts at the moment. *Flirt* has just come onboard and I—'

'Lachlan Brant is your number one priority as of

now. I'm sure you'll find a way to juggle the rest.'
Raquel stood and walked to the floor-to-ceiling windows that took in an impressive view of Melbourne's latest cultural icon, Federation Square, and the beautiful dome of Flinders Street Station. 'I have every confidence in you, Keely. If you do well, there could be a promotion in this for you.'

Great. Just great.

How could she refuse tailing Lachlan Brant's welltoned tail in exchange for a chance at the big time?

'I'll do my best.' Inwardly sighing in resignation, she knew that in the Rottie's case her best often wasn't good enough.

'See that you do. Now, bring the man in question up here and let's see if we can get him to sign on the dotted line.'

Keely nodded, managed a grin that she knew must look like a grimace, and headed back to the foyer to find her new *assignment*.

Lachlan stood as soon as she entered the reception area and his sheer presence hit her all over again. The man was serious drool material—and, by that cocky grin, boy, did he know it.

'Ready for me now?'

Ha! If he only knew how ready…

She nodded. 'Follow me.'

He did exactly that and she was aware of him every step of the way to Raquel's office. Thankfully, he didn't have a clue to her identity as a moonlighting heckler and she hoped it stayed that way.

'Your name sounds familiar. Have we met before?'

Her hand stilled on the doorknob to the Rottie's office and she gulped. So much for breathing easy.

'I don't think so,' she managed to get out, without a trace of apprehension in her voice.

'Keely is rather an unusual name. I'm sure I've heard it recently.' He fixed her with yet another piercing glare and she could almost imagine him stroking an imaginary goatee, like some Freudian professor trying to discover the meaning of life as he racked his brain to place her.

Stifling a grin at her mental image of the gorgeous psychologist in front of her even remotely resembling one of his ancient predecessors, she knocked on Raquel's door and waited for the usual barked command to enter.

'Come in.' Judging by the decibel level, Raquel was keeping it down to a dull roar in deference to Lachlan's status as prospective 'assignment' material.

'Is this a bad time?' Lachlan muttered under his breath, placing a hand in the small of her back to guide her through the door.

If she'd learned one thing it was never to slander her boss with anyone other than Emma and Tahlia, and especially not with strangers. However, with his innocuous touch burning a hole through her cool wool jacket, Keely lost all rational thought for a moment.

*Concentrate, girl.* She needed the promotion to Director of Graphic Design, and babbling in front of her boss and her newest project was not the way to go about it.

'Raquel is very busy,' she said, eagerly pushing open the door to escape the intimacy that seemed to envelop them in the deserted corridor.

'I don't speak to prospective clients like that when I'm busy,' he muttered as they entered the airy office, a slight frown marring his brow.

The Rottie bared her teeth in an attempt at smiling and shook his hand. 'Good morning, Mr Brant. Take a seat and let's get started.'

So much for pleasantries. Raquel picked up a folder and slid it across her desk.

'Call me Lachlan. And surely all this paperwork is a mere formality?' He gestured to the folder he'd barely flicked through. 'I've already done my research, and it looks like WWW Designs will suit my needs, so let's dispense with the sales pitch. I'm eager to get started straight away.'

Raquel's eyes gleamed behind her rimless glasses. She was obviously pleased at landing a big client with seemingly little effort. 'Well, that was relatively painless. Glad to see you're a decisive man, Lachlan, and I'm pleased that you've chosen our firm to handle your Internet needs. Why don't you take these documents with you, leave them with Chrystal once they're signed, and let Keely show you where she works her magic?'

*Magic?* The Rottie must really want to land the Brant account, badly.

'I'm looking forward to it.'

And, just like that, Keely had the sudden urge to bolt, promotion or not. Lachlan stared at her with a hint of speculation in his eyes and, with her imagination working overtime, she could've sworn she read more than an interest in her design skills there.

He continued, giving her valuable breathing space. 'Your company seems to offer exactly what I'm looking for.'

She tried to break eye contact with him and failed, suddenly knowing how a cobra felt, trapped under the hypnotising stare of a mongoose.

Besides, she was obviously reading more into his words. How could a man like him be remotely interested in her?

Clearing her throat, she finally managed to speak. 'If you'll follow me, we can get started now.'

The corners of his mouth twitched again, as if he was having difficulty keeping a straight face, and she could've bitten her tongue. Obviously, he had a different idea to what getting started meant.

Rather than making some wisecrack, as she had half-expected, he inclined his head and said, 'Lead the way.'

She was expecting a parting shot from Raquel, and her boss didn't disappoint. 'Make this your best work, Keely.'

Keely smiled through gritted teeth and nodded. As

if she ever produced anything less! Though the way her mind kept wandering, from the way Lachlan's suit seemed tailormade for his broad-shouldered frame to the way he smiled with his eyes as well as his mouth, maybe the Rottie had a point in reminding her to keep focused on the job at hand?

As she closed the door Lachlan asked, 'Is she always like that?'

Keely resisted the urge to growl and make like a possessive dog over a bone, the way she did with the girls when one of them had a gripe with their boss.

'Raquel is very driven. It's what keeps this company at the top,' she said, hoping that the good Lord would reward her for being so professional—with the big fat promotion she'd coveted for ages.

'Good to hear. I only work with the best.' He smiled and she noticed the fine lines fanning out from the corners of his eyes, lending a tiny flaw to the otherwise model-handsome face. He leaned towards her and for one insane moment she thought he was going to kiss her. 'And it looks like I've got it here.'

'Are you flirting with me?'

Oops! The words had popped out before she could stop them and to her horror, his smile broadened into a fully fledged grin, like that of a starving cat toying with an itty-bitty mouse.

'What if I am?'

*That would mean you're interested in me as a woman and it's my lucky day!*

Mentally slapping herself for her wayward and wishful thoughts, she said, 'That wouldn't be very professional. We have a lot of work to do and I'd rather not be distracted.'

True to her cat analogy, he pounced. 'You think I'm a distraction, huh?'

Who was the man trying to kid? In the last half-hour she'd thought about his body, eyes, smile and butt—in that order. Well, maybe the latter had been higher on the list, but it wouldn't help to think about that now, when she could hardly string two coherent words together as it was.

'Don't flatter yourself.' *I'm doing enough for the both of us.* Even if it was only in her mind. 'I merely meant that word games aren't my style. I'd rather focus on the job at hand.'

He'd fallen into step beside her and thankfully she didn't have to look at him, preferring to concentrate on the suddenly onerous task of putting one foot in front of the other and not falling flat on her face. She had an embarrassing habit of clumsiness around men who grabbed her interest and she had no intention of adding to his obvious amusement by sprawling at his feet.

'Mmm…interesting. Does that apply to all areas of your life?'

What was with this guy? He might be irresistible but didn't he ever switch off the charm?

'That's none of your business.' She pushed open

the door to her office and waved him in. 'Speaking of which, I think it's time we got down to some.'

'After you.'

She brushed past him, catching a faint waft of aftershave. She usually hated the stuff, but this was a tantalizing blend of fresh citrus that seemed to wrap around her and add to the heady sensation of being in a confined space with the hottest man to enter her sphere in a long time.

Grateful to have a seat before she made a complete fool of herself, she gestured to the one next to her. 'Let's get started.'

His knee touched hers as he folded his long legs beneath the desk, sending heat sizzling through her body and hot-wiring her dormant hormones.

Great. Not only had her mind entered meltdown mode, her body had followed suit.

'I'm all yours,' he said, sitting back and folding his arms, his confident grin setting her heart hammering in her chest.

And as she reached forward to angle the computer screen towards him and knocked over her credenza, sending pens, paperclips and rulers in all directions, she could only think of one response.

*I wish.*


Lachlan managed to appear interested as Keely prattled on about search engines, uploading pages, hosting companies and web space. However, the sultry brunette's non-verbal cues intrigued him more than anything she was saying.

From her rigid posture and fiddling fingers to her tapping foot, she seemed nervous.

And so she should be.

The sophisticated woman doing her best to impress him with her knowledge had a secret and, though he hadn't said anything yet, he was on to her.

Cops never forgot a face, and in his profession, after three years on the radio, he never forgot a voice. Though his late-night caller last week had sounded intoxicated, he remembered every cadence, every modulation of the melodious voice that had scrutinized his character and found it lacking.

He'd been angry at the time, and now that his beautiful heckler had been unexpectedly dropped in his lap, could've fired both barrels at her. However, he was in a playful mood today. Perhaps he would string her along till he felt like doing a little heckling of his own?

'Do you have any ideas about the image you want portrayed on your web page?'

She picked up a pen and tapped it against her thigh as she waited for his answer, and all he could think about was the way her hazel-coloured eyes sparkled with intelligence, how the trendy black pinstripe suit fitted her curvy body to perfection, and what he would give for another glimpse of the cheeky dimple that appeared like an unexpected bonus when she smiled.

'I've been in radio for a while. Perhaps you've listened to the Brant Show?'

*Bull's-eye!* He watched her blush, the faint pink staining her cheeks lending her face a glow, and suddenly he wondered if any other activities could bring that tinge of colour to her face.

She nodded and looked at some distant point over his left shoulder. 'I've listened to your show on the odd occasion. It's very interesting.'

'What do you think of my advice?'

To his delight, her blush deepened. 'You seem to know what you're talking about.'

The pen she held increased its staccato tempo against her thigh and, despite the fun he was having in baiting her, he decided to put an end to her obvious discomfort.

'Thanks. The producers of my prospective TV show want to capture some of my expertise from radio while adding a fresh look at the same time. Think you can help me out?'

Tucking the pen behind her ear and swivelling to face the PC monitor, she smiled and his blood pressure rocketed. God, she was beautiful—from her shoulder-length sleek chocolate-brown hair to that adorable dimple.

He hadn't dated anyone in a while, after the last disaster. His ex-girlfriend hadn't tolerated a man who worked all hours and, though he'd spent quality time with her, she'd ended the relationship after four short months.

Maybe it was time to get back into the dating scene? Starting with the lovely Keely, who had switched her attention to the screen in front of her as she navigated through a host of complex computer programs while he studied her.

'I'm sure I can help. Is this like something you had in mind?'

He glanced at the screen, surprised at the speed with which she'd conjured up a pro forma. 'Wow, you're a whiz on that thing.'

She shrugged and turned away, as if uncomfortable with his praise. 'It's what I do. If you don't like the layout or colour scheme we can change it easily, but I thought you might like this?'

She'd chosen a bold template with a black background and royal blue font—very contemporary, very eye-catching.

'I like it. I'm that easy to read, huh?'

Once again, he caught a spark in her eyes that had him itching to close the short distance between them and haul her into his arms. He'd never had caveman tendencies before, but there was something about her that just begged him to show her his club and coerce her into heading back to his cave.

She folded her hands in her lap, probably to stop them fiddling, and looked directly into his eyes. 'It's a talent I have, reading people. It helps in my job, in delivering exactly what the client is after. And you seem easier to read than most.'

'Is that so?'

She nodded, and he resisted the urge to reach out and tuck the strand of hair that swung across her face behind her ear. 'You're a successful man, determined to make it to the top of your profession. Image is everything to you and you don't like people questioning your beliefs. Well-groomed, personable, charming—it's all part of the persona.'

Oh, she was good.

'Anything else to add?'

'I know just the thing to complete the package.'

He leaned forward, eager to hear what she had to say. She'd switched to teasing mode and, with her eyes twinkling and her glossy lips curved in a semi-smile, she had him intrigued.

'What's that?'

She hit a button on the keyboard and the screen became animated with a host of fancy graphics flashing across it.

'Ta-da! The perfect website, of course.' Her proud grin sent a thrill through him. If she got this excited about her work, imagine her enthusiasm for pursuits outside the office...

He smiled, making an instant decision to take a risk.

'I like it, though there's something else that would complete the package much better.'

Her face fell for a moment, as if he'd unjustly criticized her. 'What's that?'

Before he could stop himself, he reached across, tipped her chin up with his finger and stared into her remarkable eyes. 'The perfect woman.'

# CHAPTER TWO

*'Accessorise wisely. Choose a man with as much care
as you would a handbag to go with those divine shoes.'*
*Tahlia Moran, long-time friend and expert on men.*

'WHAT happened then?' Emma leaned forward,
hanging on every word.

Keely took a sip of her sparkling mineral water
and shrugged. 'Nothing. Lucy came barging into my
office and we sprang apart like we'd been doing
something wrong.' She stabbed the last piece of let-
tuce from her Caesar salad and forked it into her
mouth.

Tahlia swivelled her head between the two of them
as if watching a Wimbledon Final. 'So you think he
was implying you're his perfect woman?'

Emma frowned and answered before Keely had a
chance. 'Of course. What else could he mean?
Besides, she said he was flirting with her before then
anyway.'

Tahlia ignored Emma's response. 'Em, you'd see
the romantic side of two ants meeting on a crack in
a footpath.'

Keely grinned as her two best friends discussed

her love life—or lack of one, more like it—as if she wasn't even there.

'Romance makes the world go round.' Emma pronounced it as a fact rather than one of her favourite theories.

'I think you mean money,' Tahlia said dryly, beckoning the waiter over to take their coffee order before they rushed back to the office.

Emma shook her head. 'Not everyone's as money-oriented as you, Miss Director of Sales.'

'I'm goal-oriented, not money-oriented. There's a difference. Nothing wrong with wanting to make it to the top.'

'What about the glass ceiling?' Keely teased, knowing her response was guaranteed to get a reaction out of Tahlia every time and thankful that the focus of the conversation had turned away from her encounter with Lachlan Brant.

Tahlia's green eyes flashed as she waved her hand in a dismissive gesture. 'No such thing, honey. I'm going places in this company, just watch me. All the way to the top.'

'Won't the Rottie have something to say about that?'

Personally, Keely had every confidence that Tahlia would make it to CEO of WWW Designs, and she couldn't wait for the day when Raquel was ousted from the top job. In fact, every employee would throw the party of the decade when that day came.

Tahlia tucked a strand of chestnut hair into her

signature topknot and made an unladylike noise akin to a snort. 'She won't have a chance to say anything. I'll muzzle her before keeping her on a short leash and locked away in her kennel.'

'Meow!' Emma made a clawing action with her perfectly manicured fingernails.

'Hey, I wouldn't be making cat noises around the Rottie. She'd eat you alive and spit out the bones for breakfast.' Tahlia wiggled her fingers in a saucy wave at Andy, their usual waiter at Sammy's, as he handed them the bill.

'I can handle Ratchet Raquel,' Emma said as all three of them leaned back in their chairs and watched Andy walk away, admiring the fit of snug denim to his butt.

'Grrr…' Tahlia growled.

'Aah…' Emma sighed.

'Mmm…' Keely allowed herself to be distracted for a moment—after all, she could appreciate a fine piece of anatomy like the next girl—before her dilemma niggled its way back into her mind.

'So what do you think I should do?' she asked, slipping her money into the folded bill without looking.

She had the same lunch at Sammy's, the hippest café-cum-bar at Southbank—Melbourne's hot spot for all things trendy—almost on a daily basis: sparkling mineral water with a twist of lemon, Caesar salad with low-fat dressing—hold the anchovies—

followed by a fruit platter for one, capped off with a skinny latte.

Though she'd come to terms with her past, the feelings associated with spending years as an overweight, lonely teenager continued to dog her and she had no intention of ever feeling like that again. The trauma of what she'd gone through when she'd finally lost weight had left a lasting impression, one that she constantly strove to ignore.

So now she had to work hard to stay in shape, unlike Emma and Tahlia who seemed to devour calories without gaining an ounce. They actually joined her in weekly Pilates classes for fun! If they weren't her best friends, she could easily hate their well-toned, under-exercised behinds.

'I think you should weigh up the pros and cons before you jump into anything.' Tahlia delved into her handbag, pulled out a newspaper and quickly flipped to the zodiac page.

'Oh, no,' Emma groaned. 'Put that away.'

Tahlia raised an eyebrow and sent Emma her best 'don't mess with me' look. 'Keeping an eye on what fate may have planned for you isn't a bad thing.' She smoothed out the paper and ran a finger down the column. '"Work brings challenges but your focus will shift to other things. Try to go with the flow."'

Emma sighed heavily.

Keely stepped in before things turned ugly, as they inevitably did when Emma questioned Tahlia's daily reading of the horoscopes. 'Your zodiac stuff seems to have helped in your professional life, but what about in the men stakes?'

Tahlia shrugged, pulling a magazine clipping, featuring monthly predictions this time, from her bag. 'Hasn't steered me wrong in the guy department so far.'

'But you haven't got a man,' Emma pointed out.

Keely had to agree, but didn't want to gang up on Tahlia. Her tall, slim friend, who never had a hair out of place, might have it together in the career department but she wasn't exactly 'out there' when it came to dating.

Tahlia sent them both a scathing look. 'That's from choice, not from lack of prospects.' She turned to Keely. 'Now, do you want to hear what you should do about the sexy psychologist or not?'

What did she have to lose? Keely hadn't had so many sparks with a guy since…well, since…ever. And, if her intuition was correct, Lachlan had been striking a few matches of his own in her office this morning.

*But what if he finds out you're the one who gave him grief on national radio?*

It wouldn't be so bad. He struck her as a guy with a sense of humour. Maybe she should come clean and tell him the truth?

Yeah, right.

Would he still be interested in her if she revealed her identity as the woman who'd called him a

Freudian fraud, a babbling psycho and a hack who dished out advice like a near-sighted agony aunt?

Somehow, in the cold light of day, she didn't think so.

Whatever Madame Tahlia and her crystal ball had to say couldn't be any worse than telling the truth.

'Okay, let me have it. What should I do?'

Tahlia pursed her lips and nodded like an all-seeing sage. '"A study or work contact could end up being someone you want to do more than just have lunch with. Embrace the goddess within you and watch them fall: your man won't be able to keep his hands off you."'

She shrugged and stuffed the cutting back in her handbag. 'So there you are.'

'But what does it mean I should do?'

'I don't know, but now you're fully informed.'

'Give me a break,' Emma muttered under her breath.

Tahlia ignored her. 'You're a Scorpio, right?'

Keely rolled her eyes and laughed. 'Libran.'

'Just kidding!' Tahlia smiled as she stood up and swung her bag over her shoulder. 'Your fate's in your hands, kiddo. It's written in the stars.'

Keely refrained from answering. None of the past horoscope predictions had come to fruition yet: she was still waiting for that promotion, she hadn't travelled in five years, and she was still waiting for a tall, dark and handsome stranger to sweep her off her feet.

'Thanks, Tahlia.' She turned to her other friend. 'Em, what do you think?'

'Honestly? I think the wise woman over here has it partially right.' Emma sent Tahlia a cheeky grin and Tahlia raised her nose in the air as if ignoring her. 'Seems like fate has dropped this amazing guy into your lap. Why don't you take a chance and see what happens? He could be the love of your life.'

Unfortunately, that was exactly what Keely was afraid of.

Keely stared at the blank piece of paper in front of her, wondering where her muse had disappeared to. Usually when she had a new client she loved to brainstorm on paper, bringing together a host of ideas and inspiration to create the final product.

In this case, the Brant file lay open on the desk to her right, the blank page on her ergonomic incline board and she didn't have a clue. The harder she tried to come up with a concept, the more her mind drifted to the man at the centre of her project and she would start fantasizing, from the way his dark hair curled around the edges of his collar to the unique blue of his eyes.

A beep on her PC indicated she had mail and she clicked on the icon to display her e-mails—anything to distract her from her wayward thoughts.

To: *KeelyR@WWWDesigns.com*
From: *Lucy-PA@WWWDesigns.com*
Subject: New talent
Sorry 2 barge in on U & LB earlier.
Wow! IMHO, he is 2 cute!
U interested?
Luce

Keely smiled, in total agreement with her assistant's 'in my humble opinion' appraisal of Lachlan, though cute wasn't the first word that sprang to mind when describing him. Try sexy, irresistible and charming.

She typed a quick response, knowing she needed to concentrate on work but grateful for the distraction. Anyway, it would be interesting to get another female's viewpoint on the subject—besides her overzealous friends, that was. If it was up to Emma and Tahlia, she'd be married to the guy already.

To: *Lucy-PA@WWWDesigns.com*
From: *KeelyR@WWWDesigns.com*
Subject:   Latest assignment
Speaking of which, working on LB website now.
By the way, LB off-limits 2 U.
Interest level rising—all in the name of business, of course! U concentrate on Aidan.
K

She had no right to warn Lucy away from Lachlan. However, she took her job seriously these days, and if the Rottie told her to shadow the man, she would.

She could shmooze with the best of them, yet somehow the thought of spending up close and personal time with her new client sent her into a tailspin—and she sure hoped she wouldn't crash and burn.

Now, if she could just come up with a novel way to approach the man, without looking too obvious, she'd be well on her way to that hard-earned promotion.

Her phone rang and she picked it up, expecting to hear Lucy's teasing tones.

'Keely, Lachlan Brant here.'

She straightened so suddenly that she almost tipped out of her chair. Silly, really—it wasn't as if he'd walked into the room or anything.

Taking a breath and aiming for casual, she said, 'Hi, Lachlan. What can I do for you?'

He hesitated for a fraction of a second and, with her overactive imagination, the pause seemed laden with promise—maybe he would tell her exactly what she could do for him and, with a bit of luck, it wouldn't involve work?

'I was wondering how the website is coming along?'

She stared at the blank page and screen in front of her, crossed her fingers and said, 'Fine. I've just been hashing around a few ideas.'

'Such as?'

Great. Though she was creative in her job, she'd never been any good thinking on the spot, and having to tell little white lies was not one of her strong suits.

'Uh...well, seeing as you're on the radio, I was thinking of focusing on you to start with. Sort of like getting to know the man behind the voice?' She silently applauded—not bad for quick thinking.

'Sounds good. That's why I'm calling, actually.'

She should've known. For a moment she'd hoped he'd been calling to keep flirting with her or, better still, maybe ask her out.

*Get real. Focus. Before he thinks you're a complete ditz.*

'I was wondering if you'd like to come out to the station tonight and take a look at where I work. You know, get a feel for what I do, maybe incorporate a few ideas into the site?' His voice dropped lower, the deep tone sending an unexpected thrill up her spine. 'Perhaps grab a coffee afterwards?'

He'd asked her out! He'd actually taken the matter of approaching him out of her hands and she couldn't be happier.

'Bring along my file and we can work on it while we have that caffeine fix.'

And, just like that, her hopes, which had soared to the heavens a moment ago, plummeted back to earth with a resounding thud.

He didn't want to stare into her eyes over the rim of a coffee mug, flirt with her over an espresso or moon over a muffin.

Uh-uh. He'd asked her to have coffee with him to *work*.

She should be rapt he'd given her an easy way to

start her assignment without having to come up with some lame excuse herself. Then why was she disappointed that his invitation had been about business and not a teensy-eensy bit of pleasure?

Instilling the right amount of enthusiasm into her voice, she replied, 'Sounds good. What time should I meet you?'

'Why don't I pick you up? The security at the station can be a bit tough on strangers, particularly for the night shift. There's a lot of crackpots out there who have nothing better to do than heckle me.'

She choked on the sip of water she'd been having, coughing and spluttering while trying to contort her arm to pat herself on the back.

'Are you okay?'

She could've sworn she heard amusement in his voice but dismissed it. What was so funny about the fact that she'd almost choked to death?

'Surely my suggestion to pick you up hasn't got you that choked up?'

'Depends on your version of picking up,' she said, wondering where that had come from.

Darn it, he'd think she was flirting with him—which she was, but why couldn't she be a whole lot more subtle about it?

'Let's start with the standard garden-variety pickup from your place and see if we can work on the other pick-up over coffee.' He chuckled, the sound of his rich, deep laughter enveloping her in its intimate cocoon, drawing her further under his spell.

And, just like that, he took up where they'd left off in her office, flirting like a pro.

She really shouldn't encourage him.

He was business.

He was a psychologist who could spend a lifetime psychoanalysing her.

He was way out of her league.

'I take your silence as agreement?'

Managing to shake herself out of her fantasy world, she said, 'It's an improvement on the choking, don't you think?'

'Nothing about you needs improving, Keely.'

She loved the way he said her name, drawing out the *ee* sound in its correct pronunciation. Many people called her Kelly and she hated it.

'Thanks. What time tonight?' She knew his show started at seven, which wouldn't give her much time to get home from work and do the usual pre-date routine.

*It's not a date,* her voice of reason screamed. And she happily ignored it.

'Is six too early?'

Heck, yes! She wouldn't have time to blow-dry her hair, pick out an outfit designed to impress and do a quick tidy up just in case he popped in afterwards.

'No problem. I live in Beacon Cove, Port Melbourne. Apartment 8/24 on the Esplanade.'

'Great. I'll see you at six.' He suddenly sounded

brisk and businesslike and she wondered if she'd just imagined the whole conversation and its undertones.

'Keely?'

'Mmm?'

'I'm looking forward to it.'

He disconnected before she had a chance to respond, which was rather fortunate as it would've been hard to answer him while grinning like a loon.

Keely barely raised her head as Lucy entered her office. She didn't have a moment to waste and, apart from having to head home and get ready, she needed to have something down on paper for Lachlan's file. Otherwise he'd know she was a total phoney. About the only ideas she'd hashed to date were about the two of them getting up close and personal, and she didn't think that would be appropriate to have on his web page, displayed for the world to see.

Lucy perched on the end of her desk, took off her rose-coloured glasses and wiped them with the end of her funky lime-green top.

'What's got you in a tizz?'

Keely placed the Brant file in her tote bag and zipped it shut. 'I have to leave. Now.'

'Hot date, huh?'

She shook her head. 'No.' And, despite her best intentions to stay cool about the evening ahead and not read anything into it, she blushed.

Predictably, her astute assistant pounced. 'You

*have* got a date! And I bet I know who it's with. Would the initials LB mean anything to you?'

'It's part of my research for his website,' Keely responded, trying not to encourage Lucy. That was all she needed—for Lucy to rev her up even more than she already was.

'Oh, right.' Lucy's eyes narrowed and she pursed her lips, as if pondering a particularly difficult puzzle. 'So that's what they're calling it these days. *Research.*'

'Luce, I haven't got time for this.' Keely picked up her bag and headed for the door. 'Besides, shouldn't you be working on the *Flirt* account?' She clicked her fingers as if remembering something. 'Speaking of Accounts, have you been down there today? I heard Aidan popped in to oversee some discrepancies.'

Keely scored a direct hit as Lucy flushed a deep crimson. 'I may have seen him briefly.'

'Why don't you ask him out? He's perfect for you.'

Lucy slid off the desk and smoothed her skirt down. 'I really must get back to work.' She stopped at the door and wiggled her fingers. 'Have fun tonight.'

'It's *work.*'

'Whatever. I'll expect an e-mail with the details of your *research* first thing in the morning. Bye.'

'It is just work,' Keely muttered under her breath as she followed Lucy out the door, wishing she could believe it.

The doorbell rang as Keely slicked gloss over her lips and took a final look in the mirror.

Not bad—black bootleg pants, burgundy fitted top, hair blow-dried to perfection and just a hint of make-up to make the most of what the good Lord had given her.

Not great, but not bad. Hopefully, Lachlan would be impressed.

As she opened the front door and his eyes lit up she had her answer.

'Hi,' was all she could manage.

If she thought he'd looked impressive at the office that morning, in suit and tie, it was nothing compared with his casual look. The combination of jeans, white T-shirt and black leather jacket had never looked so sexy on a man—and this was no ordinary man.

'You look great. Ready to go?'

She nodded, finally managing to tear her gaze away from the way the white cotton moulded to what looked like rock-hard pecs beneath.

'Just let me grab my bag,' she said, hoping that the bag was all she managed to grab in the next sixty seconds.

As if she hadn't had a hard enough time convincing herself that tonight was only about business, he had to turn up here looking like *that*.

'Nice apartment.' He stood at the door looking in

and she suddenly realised that the minute she'd caught sight of him all rational thought—along with her manners—had flown out the window.

'Come in,' she said, getting more flustered by the minute as she picked up her bag and his file slid to the floor.

Great—she must've forgotten to zip it up earlier, when she'd slid a brush and lippy for touch-ups alongside the all-important folder.

'Here, let me help.' He bent down and reached for the scattered papers at the same time she did, their heads colliding in a sickening crunch.

'Ouch!' She sank back on to the floor and rubbed her forehead, silently cursing. It looked as if her clumsy curse around cute guys had reared its ugly head again.

Thankfully, he laughed and reached out a hand to help her off the floor. 'Do I make you uncomfortable or are you always this graceful?'

'It's you,' she said, and joined in with a rueful chuckle.

'Mmm…first you up-end half your desk when I sit next to you, now you drop your bag when I get within two feet and give me a concussion in the process. It must be me.'

He pulled her up as she placed her hand in his and true to form, she stumbled against him. Totally unintentional, of course.

As she braced herself against his chest—yep, those pecs felt every bit as good as they looked—and he gazed down on her with a tender glint in his eyes, she suddenly didn't mind being such a klutz.

And when he rested his hands on her hips and smiled in that special way he had, as if she was the only woman in the world, she could've quite happily caused havoc by stumbling, upending bags and messing up desks every day of the week.

'If I'm the problem, what's the remedy?'

'You're the doc, why don't you tell me?' Her voice came out all soft and breathy while her pulse raced double-time as his hands tightened their grip, sending bolts of electricity shooting through her body.

So much for playing it cool. They hadn't even made it out of her apartment and the evening had taken on an intimate feel.

'Take two kisses and call me in the morning.'

*O-kay. Think quick. Respond with something light-hearted and witty.*

However, all she could do was stand there and stare at him while his gaze stayed riveted to her lips, as if he'd like to follow up on the first part of his advice. As he leaned forward her heart jolted at the clear intent in his eyes and she was sure the air crackled with tension around them.

*Work…assignment…client…*

The words filtered through her dazed mind and acted like an instant dampener and she reluctantly looked away.

'If that's one of your cures, I'm not surprised

you're so popular,' she murmured, managing a weak smile as her gaze fixed on his chest.

What would he think of her almost letting him kiss her? Totally unprofessional for starters, and as for the rest…

He tipped her chin up, gently forcing her to meet his stare. 'Don't second-guess yourself.'

How did he do that? She'd begun to doubt herself the minute she'd averted their near-kiss and he knew it. Despite her intoxicated ranting over the airwaves last week, he did know his stuff. And wouldn't he have a field-day if he found out why she'd been so riled about his advice to the overweight teenager that night she'd given him a verbal blast?

She opened her mouth to respond and he placed a silencing finger against it. 'And, no, I don't dish out that remedy to just anyone.'

'That's reassuring.' She aimed for brevity but her comment came out sarcastic as she pulled away from him completely, needing to establish physical distance between them to gather her thoughts.

Rather than pushing her for an explanation for her erratic behaviour—welcoming his attention one minute, freezing him out the next—as she half-expected him to do, he fixed her with a curious stare before turning away.

'As much as I'd like to cure your clumsiness, we'd better get to the station. I need to be on the air in less than an hour.' He picked up her bag and handed it to her as if nothing had happened. 'All set?'

She managed to nod, follow him out and lock up without further mishap. However, amidst her confused state at what had just occurred, one thought penetrated.

If kisses were part of his cure, she suddenly had a distinct hankering for treatment.

# CHAPTER THREE

*'Where men are concerned, always adhere to the*
*"try before you buy" policy.'*
    *Lucy, personal assistant extraordinaire.*

LACHLAN gave the console a quick once-over to
make sure he was off the air, removed his headphones and waved Keely into the booth.

He'd just spent the last three hours watching her
through the glass partition, thoroughly distracted and,
though he'd managed to present a professional front
over the airwaves, he'd had enough. It was time to
switch off and relax in the company of a woman who
sparked his interest on many levels.

He'd thought by bringing her here to the station
she might come clean about her call to him.
However, despite ample opportunity, she hadn't con-
fessed and it surprised him. He valued honesty above
all else, thanks to his lying, cheating mother, who
had left his father with a broken heart after leaching
every last ounce of devotion out of him. And he'd
vowed to never end up like his dad, a sad old man
obsessed with the one woman he couldn't have, pining away for that so-called love of a lifetime.

Though the call hadn't been a big deal in itself,

he wondered why Keely would keep it a secret, especially after the way they'd clicked.

Standing up and stretching, he knew one thing. He wanted to give this woman a chance. Apart from the sizzling attraction that arced between them whenever they got within two feet of each other, he genuinely liked her and would like to get to know her better.

Starting now.

Opening the door to the sound booth, he beckoned her in. 'What do you think? Pick up any ideas for my website?'

He watched her walk across the outer room; she was wearing a classy, understated outfit that looked as if it had been made for her. She moved with an elegance that turned heads, a quiet confidence that would make any man sit up and take notice. And he'd done that the minute he'd first laid eyes on her, strolling towards him in the foyer of WWW Designs.

Usually, he liked to ponder important decisions, but after his first glimpse of Keely he'd been ready to sign on the dotted line with the company as long as she was involved in some part of his website's production. It must've been his lucky day, for not only would she play a role in the production, she was one of the main players working with him directly.

She smiled, drawing his attention to her lips, resurrecting barely suppressed thoughts of how they'd almost connected with his earlier that evening. He hadn't meant to take things so far so fast, but had been powerless to resist her allure.

'I've looked around, spoken to a few of your co-workers and jotted down some ideas.' She picked up a pad from a nearby table and presented it to him like a proud student handing in a prized project. 'See? Enough here to keep me going for a while. Great idea to invite me to your workplace.'

He barely glanced at the pad, more interested in her non-verbal cues. Another part of his job that he couldn't turn off—he read people's unspoken actions all the time, believing they revealed a lot more about the person than first met the eye.

In this case, Keely appeared nervous as she shifted her weight from one foot to another while tapping her fingers on the back of the pad. Were her nerves a result of her little secret about heckling him or caused by something deeper? Was it just him or did all men make her this jittery?

So much for getting to know her better. It would prove extremely difficult if she reacted like a skittish filly every time he got near her.

'Glad it helped. Shall we get that coffee now?'

'Sure.' She practically bolted away from him, grabbing her bag and shoving the pad inside it before heading to the door.

'Would you like to have dinner too?' He usually didn't eat after a show, preferring to grab a light supper while planning the next day's schedule. However, the thought of staring at Keely over candlelight at his favourite seafood restaurant stimulated his appetite in more ways than one.

'I'm not hungry.' She spoke too quickly, as if the thought of sharing a meal with him was the last thing she'd want.

'Let me guess. You're on a diet.' His gaze slid over her curves as he smiled, knowing that couldn't be true. She had a stunning body, and women who looked like her knew it too.

To his amazement, she took a step back and raised her bag over her chest, as if using it like a shield, the golden flecks in her eyes glowing in what he swore was anger. 'And let *me* guess. You think I need to be on one.'

For a psychologist, he could be pretty dumb at times. Though he'd expected to make light of his dinner invitation when she'd refused it, perhaps he hadn't gone about it the best way. Many women were touchy about their weight, and though Keely had no reason to be he'd obviously hit a nerve.

He held his hands up in a friendly gesture of surrender. 'Hey, I didn't say that.'

Her eyes sparked, shooting daggers. 'Not in so many words. Though your meaning was pretty clear.'

He resisted the urge to shake his head. A minute ago he'd been wondering if it was her endearing clumsiness, her strange nervousness, her beauty or a combination of all three that had him hooked. Now, he knew he needed to re-evaluate his interest in the stunning brunette.

Looks were one thing, irrational behaviour another. And, no matter how much he'd like to get to know her better, if she showed this much paranoia over a simple comment now, there was no telling how she'd act later. He'd been burned by a woman like that in the past—his mother, the queen of inconsistency—and he'd be damned if he'd tread down that path again.

'How about we stick to our original plan for coffee and forget I ever said anything about dinner? Deal?'

To his relief, her shoulders sagged and she lowered the bag, giving him a shaky smile. 'Deal. My shout.'

And, as he followed Keely out, Lachlan knew that despite his wariness at her peculiar outburst he still had every intention of discovering what made his beautiful website designer tick.

Keely sipped at her Irish coffee, thankful for the shot of alcohol swirled through the caffeine hit. Anything to calm her nerves, which had seemed to be working overtime since the minute she'd laid eyes on Lachlan this evening. First she'd practically invited his kiss at her apartment, and then she'd made a prize fool of herself by exploding over his diet comment at the station. And, though he'd done his best to put her at ease, she knew it would be hard recovering from two *faux pas* like that in one night.

Even now, the harder she tried to act nonchalant, as if that almost-kiss back at her apartment hadn't happened, the more wound up she got. At least she hadn't dropped anything, stumbled or tripped over in the last few hours. Though he found it amusing the way she reacted around him, it embarrassed her more than she let on.

'Okay, let me have it.'

'Pardon?' Startled out of her reverie, she looked up at him and wondered how she could survive the next hour.

When he'd mentioned coffee to mull over his file, he'd omitted the part about bringing her to Melbourne's hottest new jazz club. Located not far from her office in Southbank, and sprawled over half a block, the Swing Room offered its patrons everything from soulful crooning in several lounges to intimate tables for two in a quieter area reserved for late-night sojourns.

It would've been hard enough pretending this meeting was business at an average, run-of-the-mill café. Here, with the faint sounds of a master saxophonist filtering through the speakers, the dimly lit room just barely illuminated by candles strategically placed on the tables and the rich aroma of speciality coffees lingering in the air, Keely had no hope.

The atmosphere reeked of intimacy, and the man sitting on her right with his knee occasionally brushing hers wasn't helping matters.

He made casual conversation as if they were old friends, putting her at ease with his witty anecdotes about the radio business. However, the more she focused on what he was saying, the more she noticed his lips, which led her thoughts down a completely different path altogether…

'Let me see what you've done so far.'

Hoping that he wouldn't see through her, and notice that her notes had been compiled in under half an hour at the office, she took out his file from her bag and laid it on the table.

'This is only the early stages, where I tend to brainstorm, so it probably looks a bit of a mess.'

Understatement of the year. She'd covered a single sheet of paper with over a dozen Post-It notes, jotting down the few ideas that had sprung to mind when she'd finally managed to concentrate on the task at hand.

'And don't forget that I've gained a whole lot more info from being at the station tonight, so I'll try to incorporate a few more ideas into the basic plan tomorrow.'

Unfortunately, some of the info she'd learned earlier at the station hadn't been all good. She'd let her attraction for the man cloud her judgement; yet with his inadvertent swipe at her weight he'd reminded her in no uncertain terms that he was just like the rest of the male population: obsessed by superficialities like a woman's body shape rather than considering the heart on the inside. She'd copped more than her fair share of fat jokes and snide remarks over the years and, though they'd hurt at the time, none had surprised her as much as Lachlan's dig. She'd expected more from a man like him, which just went to show that he wasn't so perfect after all. Once again, her judgement when it came to the male species was way off and she'd do a darn sight better remembering it. Besides, Lachlan Brant was business and she had no right to even contemplate acting on the attraction that sparked between them.

She resisted the urge to nibble on a fingernail as he perused the file, his face unreadable.

'Uh-huh,' were the only two syllables he uttered as he screwed up his eyes, obviously trying to make sense of her tiny scrawling on the notes.

Just when she was ready to grab her notes and flee, he looked up and smiled. 'I like what you've done so far. Creative, interesting, effective.'

He handed her the file and she wanted to hug him. Her work was her pride and joy and she lapped up praise. Raquel wasn't huge on giving her employees any pats on the back. Not that it usually mattered; Keely's work spoke for itself and her clients were quick to show their appreciation for her efforts.

'If this is what you can do in one day, I can't wait to see the finished product.' He sat back and draped an arm across the back of the chair, his hand resting merely inches from her neck.

The simple action drew her attention to the way the cotton of his T-shirt stretched across his chest, defining a host of muscles just begging to be touched.

She swallowed, desperate for the slightest amount of moisture to wet her throat, which had gone dry the second her mind associated 'muscles' and 'touching' in the same sentence.

'With your input, I'm sure I can come up with something that is suitable,' she said, trying to ignore the fact that if she leant back a fraction his fingers would brush the nape of her neck.

'Sounds good. Now that the business part of this evening is settled, let's have some fun.'

*Oh, no.* The word 'fun' had the same devastating effect on her psyche as 'muscles' and 'touching'.

'Fun?' she managed to say, though it came out more a squeak than a word.

'You don't mind if we spend a little longer here, just chilling out? I've had a rough week and wouldn't mind unwinding with good music, great coffee and even better company.' He leaned closer a fraction, his eyes beseeching her to agree, while a faint waft of his aftershave washed over her, shattering the last of any lingering doubts.

As if she needed any convincing.

'I'd like that.'

Like it? She'd *love* it. Spending time with a guy like Lachlan would be amazing, and so much more inviting than curling up in bed with her usual thriller, alone and scared half to death. Though she read scary novels by choice, she still hadn't conquered her fear whenever she heard a noise while doing so.

'Good, that's settled. Would you like another drink?'

'A latte would be fine, thanks.'

He raised an eyebrow. 'You sure? All that caffeine is guaranteed to keep you up all night.'

She shrugged. 'I'm a poor sleeper anyway.' Painful memories could do that to a person, as much as she tried to block them out.

'That's too bad. Maybe you haven't tried the right nightcap?'

'I've tried them all. Hot milk, camomile tea, valerian, counting sheep, listening to ocean sounds and heartbeat lullabies. Nothing works.' She refrained from adding that the only time she did manage to get a decent night's sleep was when she'd been involved in a relationship and had the comforting warmth of a male body next to her.

'I might have just the thing for you.'

*Oh, I certainly hope so,* a naughty voice inside her head whispered, and she deliberately ignored it. 'What's that?'

He leaned closer and lowered his voice, a secretive smile playing about his lips. 'I'm not sure if you'd be up for it.'

The effect of his smile was instant, her pulse picking up tempo and keeping rhythm with her pounding heart. 'Why don't you let me be the judge of that?'

His smile broadened to a grin. 'It involves you lying down, me being next to you and opening your mind to a host of possibilities.'

*Oh, boy.* She gulped, desperately wishing for something fabulously witty to say. Instead, her mind was a complete blank, apart from the erotic images that filtered across it like a classic movie on constant re-run.

'I'm talking about hypnotherapy,' he said, his soft chuckle making her want to hit him.

'I knew that.'

'Really?' He captured her hand in his before she knew what was happening. 'It looks to me like you had something more…*interesting* in mind.'

She struggled to concentrate on the simple task of speaking while his thumb gently brushed the back of her hand and created havoc in the process.

'I'm not that easy to read.'

'Oh, no?'

The warmth of his hand, combined with the excited glint in his eyes, ignited a fire deep in her belly that spread like quicksilver through her body.

In one short day this man had elicited responses within her that she'd never experienced and never dreamed of having. A confirmed realist, she knew that the whole 'settle down with a nice steady boy, get married, have kids and live in the burbs' fantasy wasn't for her. How could it be, when she couldn't provide one of the vital ingredients in that happily-ever-after scenario?

Right now, she had a career to build, a promotion to gain and a whirlwind social life. Did she have room in her life for a man, a relationship and the possible implications?

He might enjoy a light-hearted affair, but what if he hoped for permanence? She'd have to walk away at the end, resulting in devastation yet again. Despite what they initially said, most men wanted children— part of their quest to prove something to the world— and she couldn't provide that.

She'd learned the hard way—Jon, the only man she'd fallen for enough to contemplate a future with, had run a million miles when she'd had the courage to tell him the truth. She'd been expecting an engagement ring; she'd ended up with more pain than it was worth.

If there was one thing she'd learned—through her overweight, low self-esteem teenage years, the gruelling hours of counselling, the dramatic weight loss and subsequent collapse—it was to protect her heart. Having it bruised, trampled and shattered did nothing for her ego, not to mention her health.

No, this time she'd be more careful.

If Lachlan Brant wanted to flirt with her, fine.

If he wanted to charm her, hold her hand and prescribe the occasional kiss, fine.

If he wanted anything else…Lord help her!

# CHAPTER FOUR

*'A man will halt your climb up the corporate ladder quicker than his exit at the first hint of the L word.'*
Raquel Wilson, all-round cynic and closet man-hater.

'WHAT'S *Keely's Collection* doing out of mothballs?' Emma picked up the scrapbook from Keely's desk and started flipping through it.

'Lucy asked me to bring it in. We're working on a quiz format for *Flirt*, and she asked if I kept any of that stuff.' Keely didn't look up from her PC screen, eager to put the finishing touches to the athletic company's web page before shifting her attention to her latest, and most distracting, client.

'This is amazing. I can't believe you call this a scrapbook. It should be a girl's handbook on surviving the dating scene.' Emma continued to flick pages. 'You've collected quotes and quizzes like most people collect stamps or postcards.'

Keely didn't look up, her concentration not wavering. Pity she couldn't do the same when it came to the Brant account. 'It's a hobby.'

Suddenly Emma let out a squeal. 'Oh, my God, you've even got stuff *I've* said about guys written in here.'

'Nobody's safe,' Keely muttered. 'Now, shut up and let me finish this.'

Emma peered over Keely's shoulder. 'Why are you hell-bent on finishing this today anyway? I thought it wasn't due till next week? I'm nowhere near completion with the animation yet.'

'Too much work,' Keely said, her fingers flying over the keyboard as she typed the last subtitles on to the site.

'Looks good,' Emma said. 'Though you being in such a hurry to finish this wouldn't have anything to do with a spunky new client, would it?'

'Don't be silly. I give all my clients equal billing.'

'Is that why you went to the Swing Room with Lachlan Brant last night? Intending to add some musical accompaniment to his website, huh?'

To her annoyance, Keely felt heat creep into her cheeks. 'How did you know?'

'A certain young woman whose lips are as loose as her morals told me.'

'Chrystal was there?'

*Oh, great.* Now the whole office would know about her and Lachlan and would want to know details.

'The hottest new spot in town, according to our resident man-eater.' Emma perched on the edge of her desk. 'So, how was it?'

'It was just part of this whole stupid assignment business,' Keely said, trying not to remember the way Lachlan had stared at her during the latter part of the evening, the look in his eyes spelling danger for her peace of mind.

'Sure thing. In that case, you won't be interested in this.' Emma waved a piece of paper under her nose.

'What's that?' Keely tried to snatch it out of her hand and Emma raised it higher.

'Mmm…let me see. It's titled "My Perfect Man" and it fell out of your scrapbook.'

'Give me that!'

'Uh-uh, not so fast.' Emma leaped off the desk, held the paper at arm's length and started reading. 'Looks like a checklist. I wonder how many criteria the wonderful Mr Brant fits.'

Keely groaned and shook her head. 'I wrote that when I was nineteen. Can't you leave a girl in peace?'

Emma ignored her and continued. 'According to this, your perfect man would be over six feet tall, have dark hair, blue eyes, a nice smile, a sense of humour, a professional job, a great body, be adventurous, love jazz, appreciate food—read doughnuts— and be a skilled kisser.' She paused for a second, exhaled and rolled her eyes. 'Phew! Not asking for much, are you?'

'It's just a dumb list,' Keely said, remembering the exact day she'd written it.

She'd finally got her life back on track after losing all that weight and collapsing, and the first guy she'd dated, Ray the Rat, had ditched her after three months for a seventeen-year-old. The list had encapsulated every quality that Ray didn't have at the time and, hence, everything she wanted in a man.

Emma smiled. 'That's where you're wrong. I think this list details quite specifically your perfect man and, if I'm not mistaken, it seems you've already found him.'

Heat flooded Keely's cheeks. Strangely enough, she'd been thinking along similar lines as Emma read the list out. It seemed as if Lachlan met every one of her criteria, though she didn't know about the adventurous stuff yet, and she couldn't imagine him pigging out on doughnuts, not with his buffed body. As for his skill in the kissing department, she'd prefer not to go there—not with their near miss still fresh in her mind.

'I don't have time for this,' Keely said, knowing that the more Emma interrogated her about Lachlan, the more she'd want to dissect every look, word and touch from last night. And she didn't want to do that. He was business, attraction or not.

'Pity.' Emma shrugged, slid the checklist back into the scrapbook and placed it on Keely's desk. 'To be that clear on what you want in a guy and then turn your back on him when he walks into your life. Seems a shame to me.'

'Don't you have work to do?' Keely picked up the scrapbook and shoved it into her top drawer, hoping that the old adage 'out of sight, out of mind' might work in this case.

'Sure. See you after work at Pilates class?'

Keely nodded and waited till her friend had left the room before staring at the closed top drawer as if it contained a poisonous snake.

'Perfect man, my butt,' she muttered, returning her attention to the screen in front of her and wishing Lachlan Brant was anything but.

'Can I help you, Mr Brant?'

Lachlan managed to maintain eye contact with the voluptuous receptionist of WWW Designs, whose name eluded him, which was no mean feat considering she had enough cleavage on show to tempt a saint.

'Is Keely free at the moment? I'd like to have a word with her.'

In fact, he wanted to have more than a word with her, but the rest would have to wait. Ever since that almost-kiss last night, his mind had been plagued by images of her—the way she'd looked with her eyes locked on his, how she'd swayed towards him, how she'd sighed softly as she pulled away. Frankly, he'd been able to think of little else, and the only way to gain some peace of mind was to tackle the 'problem' head-on.

The woman had got under his skin in one day, a record when it came to a man who played his emotions close to his chest. He never fell for a female that quickly, even one as spectacular as Keely Rhodes. Thankfully, they'd got past that little 'moment' after his shift had ended quite quickly, and had moved into an easygoing camaraderie over coffee at the Swing Room, leaving him wondering if he'd imagined her angst.

Either way, he'd put his niggling doubts behind him for now and was eager to see where they went from here.

'I'll check if Keely's free.' The receptionist punched a few buttons on a console and spoke discreetly into a headset.

She'd better be free, in all senses of the word. The fact that Keely might have a significant other in her life hadn't crossed his mind and, though she didn't seem the type to encourage him while involved with another man, one never knew. Look at his mum.

'Keely will see you in her office now. Would you like one of these?' The receptionist held up a plate of cinnamon doughnuts that smelled delicious, somehow making the innocuous question sound as if she was offering more.

He'd had his fair share of women throw themselves at him, yet he'd always preferred the more subtle charms of a woman who acted as if she didn't possess any compared with her overtly voracious counterparts.

However, that didn't mean he had to be rude. He smiled and took one of the doughnuts. 'Thanks. Let's hope it doesn't go straight to my hips.'

'Nothing wrong with your hips from where I'm sitting,' he heard the receptionist mutter before she plastered a professional smile on her expertly made-up face and turned away to answer an incoming call.

*Let's hope the beautiful Miss Rhodes thinks so,* he thought as he half demolished the doughnut before knocking on her door.

'Come in.'

He pushed the door open, wondering how Keely would act after last night. Would she pretend nothing had happened between them or would she make a joke of it? Personally, he hoped she'd had as good a time as he had and would want to repeat the experience.

'Hope you're not too busy. Thought I might run a few ideas past you for the website...' He trailed off at the stunned look on her face. 'What's wrong?'

Keely tried not to stare, but the sight of Lachlan eating a cinnamon doughnut, one of the few criteria for the perfect man she'd assumed he wouldn't possess, floored her.

As if it wasn't bad enough he had to match every other quality on her checklist!

Pulling herself together, she managed to say, 'You like doughnuts?'

A sheepish smile spread across his handsome face. 'It's a weakness.' He shrugged, looking like a cheeky schoolboy rather than a renowned psychologist. 'What can I say?'

*You can say something rude or obnoxious again, something designed to push me away.*

However, she knew it was useless. Falling for a

guy like Lachlan—the perfect man, according to her stupid checklist—seemed inevitable.

So much for being a realist.

When it came to her heart, it was ironic that she could be as gullible as Emma, a true romantic.

'Do I have sugar covering my lips or something?'

She bit back her first retort of *or something; preferably me.* 'Sorry if I appeared distracted. I was in the middle of all this.'

'And here I was, hoping that I was the distraction.' He smiled, the simple action illuminating his face. She'd never known a guy to smile like that, his eyes lighting up as if the world was a great place to be. If she was truly delusional, she'd like to think that she had that effect on him.

'You are.' The words popped out and his grin broadened. 'I mean, I was putting the finishing touches on another client's site, and now I need to switch my thinking to you.'

Lame, even by her standards, and by the amused look on his face he didn't buy it for a minute.

'Did you enjoy last night?'

*Oh, heck.* Was he referring to the radio station, the jazz club or the physical attraction that had zinged between them?

Rather than come up with more pathetic excuses, she decided to keep her answer simple. 'Yes, I did.'

'Good. It makes what I have to suggest now all the more appropriate.'

*Oh-oh.* The only suggestions he could possibly

make that sprang to mind were highly inappropriate and she could only wish.

'Sounds interesting,' she said, resisting the urge to swing on her chair. Knowing her luck around him, she'd lean back too far and fall off it.

'It is. How would you like to gain real insight into the man behind the voice and put a few masterful touches on my website in the process?'

'I thought that was what last night was about?'

'It was only the start. What I had in mind was you spending time with me in various aspects of my life, watching me interact in different situations, getting a feel for what I want on my website. Look at it as a way to gain firsthand knowledge of what makes Lachlan Brant tick.'

Keely struggled to maintain a calm façade while she composed her thoughts. Funnily enough, she had been about to suggest something similar, though hadn't quite come up with the right words to approach him. This assignment was important to her and she'd make it the best work she'd done if it killed her—though with a guy like Lachlan by her side 24/7, what a way to go.

'Let me get this straight. I get to spend time with you away from work to gain insight into your personality? What situations did you have in mind?'

He crossed his arms, drawing her attention to his broad shoulders and the way his pale blue business shirt stretched across them. 'I like to surf, bushwalk and barbecue to chill out and de-stress, so I thought you could hang out with me, ask some in-depth questions, make a few notes.'

He strode across the room, closing the distance between them in an instant, and crouched down next to her. 'All strictly professional, of course.'

She inhaled deeply, trying to get oxygen to her befuddled brain in a hurry. Instead, his aftershave tempted her to lean closer to him and savour the crisp, clean smell that blended with his pheromones to entice her further.

To make matters worse, he stared at her with an intensity that took her breath away.

'Call it research.' He rested his hand on the back of her chair.

She cleared her throat, wishing he'd stop looking at her like that. How was a girl supposed to think with the bluest eyes she'd ever seen glued to her? 'Sounds good. Do you have any of that adventurous stuff planned for this weekend?'

He laughed, and the spell that enveloped them cleared in a second. 'Not into the outdoors, huh?'

Not unless it involved cuddling under a blanket on a windswept beach with the man of her dreams. As if that was going to happen in a hurry! 'What gave it away?'

'The frown, the way you wrinkled up your nose. Didn't I tell you I'm an expert on body language?'

*Girl, don't go there!* A host of wicked responses sprang to mind about exactly how he could read her body—by touch, being the primary choice—and she bit back every one of them.

What had got into her? Her hormones were clouding her judgement. She wasn't supposed to like the man, remember? He professed the same textbook psychobabble as the rest of his profession; he had dished out his baloney to that overweight teenager as if he knew how the poor girl felt.

*Yeah, right.* Since when had a guy who looked like him ever sought solace in food, gorging on sweet things to fill the empty void in his life? Try never. He wouldn't have a clue about being unpopular because of one's size, or the accompanying feelings of embarrassment, worthlessness and soul-destroying loneliness.

His caller that night had been reaching out to him, probably plucking up what meagre supply of courage she possessed to ring him, and what had he done? He had given the girl a two-minute quick fix, incorporating the standard line about joining a gym, exercising more, eating less and making new friends.

Keely's heart had bled for the girl. She'd been there, done that and burnt the T-shirt a long time ago. Hearing Lachlan's trite advice, no matter how good his intentions, had sparked her into reaching for her mobile and giving him the verbal spray he'd deserved.

As for her reaction to his diet comment last night, guys with buffed bods who looked as if they'd stepped off the cover of a magazine shouldn't go there. Ever.

Logically, she shouldn't be attracted to him. She'd never measure up. Physically, she wanted to get as close as she could and stay there for the remainder of her assignment.

'Hey, I won't make you jump off any cliffs or anything. You can just sit back and watch.' Concern had replaced interest in his eyes and she wrenched her attention back to the present, slamming the door on her self-esteem issues, wishing she could lock it and throw away the key for ever.

'Fine. I'll be in touch. Now, I really have to get back to it.'

Though she wasn't fine. Not by a long shot.

And she had a feeling that the more time she spent in Lachlan's company, the more the protective wall she'd built around her heart could crumble, one brick at a time.

# CHAPTER FIVE

*'It doesn't matter if he has two left feet as long as he's
an expert at horizontal folk-dancing.'*
                                      *Chrystal, serial man-eater.*

'YOU two are dating,' Tahlia muttered under her
breath as she stretched forward, her head almost
touching her knee.

'Spending time together as part of a work assignment doesn't constitute dating,' Keely said, wishing
the Pilates class could go on for ever. That way, she
wouldn't have to think about Lachlan Brant and the
chaos he'd turned her life into. Concentrating on her
aching muscles proved an excellent distraction, for
all of two seconds.

Emma stood in one smooth movement and held
out her hand to pull Keely up. 'But it's more than
work. What about the flirting? And all this time
you'll be spending together as research? Don't forget
it was his idea, even though you were going to suggest it anyway.'

Keely had been pondering the very same question
all day and, though she'd managed to finish the bulk
of her work, her mind had constantly drifted to
Lachlan and the way he made her feel in his pres-

ence—uncertain, excited, like being on a rollercoaster and not knowing when the next exhilarating plummet would be.

She'd tried to ignore her erratic hormones and focus on work. Nadia had finally announced her pregnancy and Keely was sure it was no coincidence that Raquel had entrusted this account to her. If she succeeded in satisfying Lachlan Brant as a client, she had a sneaking suspicion the promotion was hers.

'It's just that. Research. I learn more about the man; his website will reflect my efforts. Obviously, he wants it to be top-notch too; that's why he came up with the idea for me to spend time with him.'

Tahlia finished her stretch and stood, taking a deep slug from her water bottle. 'I know this promotion is important to you but don't kid yourself. This man has the hots for you and, if I'm not mistaken, the feeling is entirely mutual.'

Keely hated it when her friends were right.

'So? What's wrong with having a little fun? It's not going to affect my work. In fact, it's going to enhance it.'

Emma lifted her long blonde ponytail, draped a towel across her neck and smiled. 'Sweetie, there's nothing wrong with having fun. I just think there's more to it than that. If the guy was only interested in a quick roll in the sack, he wouldn't be going to all this trouble.'

Expecting an argument from the ever-practical Tahlia, Keely looked at her.

To her surprise, Tahlia shrugged. 'Sorry, I have to agree with the romantic one on this.'

'Great,' Keely said, 'that's all I need. You two agreeing for once.'

'We're just being objective.' Emma handed her a sports drink and Keely drank deeply, hoping the electrolytes would help replenish some of the brain cells she seemed to have lost since she'd first laid eyes on Lachlan.

'Which is probably difficult in your case, seeing as he keeps finding excuses to see you. Must be terribly distracting.' Tahlia grinned and tossed her empty drink bottle into a nearby bin.

'Remind me never to tell you two another detail about my love life.' Keely slung her gym bag over her shoulder and headed for the showers.

'Love life?' Emma pounced on the words once they left her mouth as the girls fell into step beside her.

Keely bit back a groan. She shouldn't blame her friends for encouraging her. She was doing enough fairy tale building in her own head.

'Okay, you got me. I like the guy. He's perfect. There. Satisfied?'

'Not as much as you're going to be if Lucky Lachlan has his way with you over the weekend away,' Tahlia said, trying her best to look innocent while holding the door to the locker room open.

Emma giggled and Keely rolled her eyes, a small part of her hoping that her friend's prediction would come true.

Lucy's e-mail was the first Keely opened on Friday morning and, unfortunately, it didn't help her frame of mind.

To: *KeelyR@WWWDesigns.com*
From: *Lucy-PA@WWWDesigns.com*
Subject: The Perfect Man
K,
Have completed formulating quiz for *Flirt* site.
*Keely's Collection* was inspirational 4 the perfect man quiz.
Thought U might like to check out my work?
Maybe apply questions to LB, your PM, and get the answers back to me?
Luce

She stifled a groan. Not Lucy too! Emma and Tahlia egging her on were bad enough, now she had her trusty assistant on the case.

Quickly scanning the list of quiz questions, she couldn't help but chuckle.

The Perfect Man's most desirable asset is:
a) great pecs
b) great biceps
c) great butt
d) great 'package'

Does the Perfect Man prefer:
a) boxers
b) jocks
c) thongs
d) free-balling it

The Perfect Man looks best in:
a) a suit
b) jeans
c) underwear
d) nothing at all

The Perfect Man's best accessory is:
a) his cuff-links
b) his Palm Pilot
c) his tie-pin
d) you

Though she was tempted to answer 'd' to all of the above for a laugh, she typed a quick response.

To: *Lucy-PA@WWWDesigns.com*
　From: *KeelyR@WWWDesigns.com*
　Subject: The PM fallacy
Luce,
In my case, no such thing.

Nice work, though. Perhaps applying these questions to Aidan might be more appropriate?
Isn't he your PM?
K

For someone who loved her scrapbook, and who had enjoyed jotting down quotes from her favourite people her entire life, she suddenly wished she'd ditched *Keely's Collection* for a more practical guide. Perhaps something like *Real Men Aren't Perfect. Evaluate every relationship you've ever had and find out why.*

She'd devised her checklist as a tongue-in-cheek exercise when dumped by Ray all those years ago, though she'd forgotten to apply it when Jon had come along four years later and she'd really fallen hard. Maybe if she'd remembered it she wouldn't have gone through the heartache of losing a man she'd thought she loved at the time. She'd also realised that if a guy who'd openly professed his love for her could then run out on her after discovering her inability to have kids—then any man could.

Now, the fictitious man she'd described in her list had walked into her life. From his dark wavy hair and bluer-than-blue eyes to his fondness for doughnuts, he appeared perfect in every way.

And what was she going to do about it?

'Damned if I know,' she muttered as she scanned a few inter-office memos.

Lucy's response came in just as she'd deleted the last one.

To: *KeelyR@WWWDesigns.com*
From: *Lucy-PA@WWWDesigns.com*
Subject: R all the good ones taken?
K,
Aidan is an accountant, therefore can't be PM material
Luce

Shaking her head, she wondered when Lucy was going to wake up, take off her rose-coloured glasses—literally—and take a good look at what was right in front of her. Aidan seemed an ideal match for her and, though he appeared conservative at first glance, she knew he harboured a wild streak. After all, she'd seen the car he drove, and a maroon convertible sports car with cream leather seats didn't seem too boring to her.

Add to that the abseiling equipment she'd glimpsed in the rear seat and there were definite possibilities there.

The guy seemed to have it all—good looks, a great job, he was polite and genuinely interested in Lucy. What more did the girl need?

Promising herself this would be the last e-mail she sent before settling down to work for the day, she responded.

To: *Lucy-PA@WWWDesigns.com*
From: *KeelyR@WWWDesigns.com*
Subject: Perish the thought!
Luce,
That makes him into figures. Particularly yours if
I'm not mistaken.
Your PM is due in today.
Y don't U follow up?
K
(PS Get back to work!)

Taking a leaf out of her own book, she clicked on
the icon to bring up Lachlan's website and hoped she
could focus on work and not on the weekend ahead.
Though the logical part of her brain knew that spending time with Lachlan at his beach house was work,
she had a sneaking suspicion that her romantic side
was telling her otherwise.

Keely had watched Lachlan ride monstrous waves
perched on an impossibly small piece of fibreglass
for the last hour, her heart pounding most of the time.

However, it was nothing compared to the way it
thundered in her chest as he jogged up the beach
towards her.

The water-slicked wetsuit moulded to him like a
second skin, delineating every last muscle of his
toned body as he carried the surfboard under one arm
as if it weighed nothing at all. He'd run a hand

through his hair, sending dark spikes in all directions, while the deep blue of his eyes reflected the cloudless Torquay sky.

As he got closer his boyish grin lit a fire within her, its heat licking along every nerve-ending in her body, heightening her awareness till nothing else existed but this man, this moment.

'So, what do you think?' He planted the surfboard in the sand and leaned against it, looking like an irresistible advertisement for the sport.

'I think you're nuts for balancing on that little board and inviting the sharks to nibble at your toes.'

His smile broadened. 'Care to try?'

'The balancing or the nibbling?' The words popped out before she could stop them and his smile turned to laughter.

'I didn't know you had a foot fetish. Lucky I'm a psychologist.'

She rolled her eyes, enjoying the light-hearted banter they'd been trading all day. The drive from Melbourne to Bell's Beach had taken just over an hour, and her initial nervousness at spending so much time confined in his car had vanished as they'd made small talk.

'Then colour me crazy.'

He squatted down beside her, effectively blocking out the sun, and tucked a strand of hair behind her ear. 'Care for an in-depth one-on-one consultation?'

His voice dropped lower, its tone seductively

husky, and she knew without a shadow of a doubt that he wasn't offering her a professional evaluation.

She leaned back on her outstretched arms in an attempt to put some distance between them. If she'd been hot before, having him this close ensured she entered meltdown.

'Maybe I'm too complicated for you to figure out?'

'Maybe I like a challenge?'

'Is that what I am to you?'

He shook his head, showering her in a fine spray of seawater droplets, a welcome relief of cool against her fiery cheeks. Whatever made her think she could match wits with this man, trade quips with him like an experienced flirt?

Though she prided herself on being a savvy city girl, she was still an inexperienced amateur when it came to the male sex.

'You're an intriguing woman, Keely Rhodes. One I'd like to get to know a whole lot better.' He tilted her chin up and brushed his thumb along her bottom lip, his gaze locked on hers.

'We're here to work, not socialise,' she blurted out, eager to say anything to distract herself from the hypnotic intensity of his stare or the way her lips still tingled after his brief contact. 'Isn't that what you had in mind when we initially discussed this?'

She expected him to break eye contact, look guilty and lie through his teeth.

Instead, he surprised her.

'Why can't we do both? I thought you'd gain valuable knowledge for the website by spending time with me. You know, give it a personal touch.' He captured her hand in his, intertwining fingers in a possessive gesture that quietly thrilled her. 'However, I admit to wanting more from the weekend.'

'I'm not going to sleep with you.' She pronounced it more as a statement to convince herself rather than a warning to him.

Instead of dropping her hand, he tightened his hold. 'Wow, some guy really did a number on you, didn't he?'

To her annoyance, she blushed. Now wasn't the time or place to talk about her disastrous history with men, her self-esteem problem and the ensuing damage it had caused. If she got started, he'd be compelled to charge her by the hour! Besides, psychologists hadn't been her favourite people following long and tiresome hours spent in counselling and, though her hormones were clouding her judgement when it came to this guy, she had no intention of losing her wits completely and trusting him.

'I'd rather not talk about it.'

To her relief, he nodded. 'Fine, then I'll talk and you listen. I'm not one of your slick city guys. Sure, I like Melbourne and its vibe, but I'm a country boy at heart. I love the fresh air, the bush, the ocean.' He gestured to the vista behind him as if reinforcing his words. 'I'm not into lies or pretence. I value honesty above all else, and when I like something I acknowledge it.'

Rather than soothing her, his words sliced into her heart. Honesty? Great. What would he say if she revealed her secret to him?

*Which one?* a tiny voice in her head prompted— the fact that you heckled him and slandered his professional character or the one you use to push away every man who tries to get close to you?

'And I like you. That's what this is all about.'

She swallowed, buoyed by his refreshing attitude and terrified beyond belief. No man had ever been that up-front with her. And it scared her. A lot.

Searching for the right words to deflect his attention—which she liked way too much—she bumbled along in predictable fashion. 'I'm flattered, but right now I need to focus on my career. I haven't got time for anything else in my life. I'm thinking business and you're—'

'Thinking pleasure?' he interrupted, raising her hand to his mouth and nibbling on her fingertips with small, precise nips.

'Mmm...' She sighed and closed her eyes for a moment, instantly forgetting all the reasons why she shouldn't be doing this.

'Stop analysing and just feel,' he murmured, the soft touch of his mouth against her palm sending bolts of electricity shooting up her arm.

Suddenly her voice of reason gave her a big, loud wake-up call—*so much for business*—and she pulled her hand away before he could undermine her stance to keep things between them strictly professional any more than he already had. 'That's rich coming from you, the king of analysis.'

He shrugged. 'Work's work. You and me, that's something else entirely.'

She took a deep breath, hoping a lungful of sea air would clear her mind, for the longer he stared at her as if she was the only woman in the world for him, the harder it was for her to respond.

'I'm not sure what you want from me,' she said, making a lightning-quick decision to tell him exactly how she was feeling. He wanted honesty? She'd give it to him, at least for the moment.

'I want a website.' He smiled, obviously trying to lighten the mood.

'And?' she persisted, unable to shake the feeling that they'd reached an important crossroad in their brief relationship. *Working relationship*, that is.

She didn't have time for mix-ups or games. If he wanted more from her than a fabulous website, now was the time for him to speak up. And for her to run for the hills as she usually did.

His grip on her hand tightened. 'I want to get to know you better. Nothing more, nothing less. Think you can handle that?'

'As long as we don't lose sight of the real reason I'm here. And that's to work.'

Despite her false bravado, a small part of her was scared out of its wits.

She could listen to her self-talk about *He's work, he's a means to an end, he's the best opportunity for that promotion you've ever had.*

However, what would happen if she switched off the rational, clear-thinking voice inside her head and followed her heart for once?

While spending the weekend away, with him in her face all the time, it didn't bear thinking about.

# CHAPTER SIX

*'Is a sensitive, considerate man: a) a myth,*
*b) an oxymoron, c) a moron?'*
*Lucy, looking for Mr Right in all the wrong places.*

LACHLAN flipped the steaks on the barbecue and watched Keely rustle up a salad through the kitchen window. Even with a slight frown marring her brow as she concentrated on getting the right mix of olive oil, lemon and balsamic vinegar, she looked beautiful.

He'd had a hard time concentrating on riding the waves earlier that afternoon, his mind wandering to the woman sitting on the pristine sand, watching him. He'd almost been wiped out several times but had rallied at the last moment, only to be wiped out in earnest when he'd finished surfing and seen the look in her eyes as he jogged up the beach towards her.

She'd looked at him like a woman starved, with her eye on the entrée, main course and dessert all rolled into one. He'd been flattered. Hell, he'd been ready to rip off his wetsuit and take her right then and there in the sand, discomfort be damned.

However, Keely had secrets, and not just the one about her being his late-night heckler. He'd glimpsed

81

vulnerability, uncertainty, and what he could almost label fear in her eyes whenever he mentioned his interest in her.

Not that he'd pushed too hard yet. He wasn't a complete fool. Sure, he wanted to get to know her better, but he had a feeling that if he rushed her she would bolt quicker than his mum had at the first offer from one of her numerous lovers.

'By the look on your face, this barbecuing business is serious stuff.'

Quashing the sharp stab of pain that memories of his traitorous mother never failed to raise, he brandished the stainless steel tongs at her. 'It is. Wouldn't want you to complain about the rump being too rare.'

To his delight, she sent a pointed look at his butt and raised an eyebrow. 'Nothing wrong with a bit of rare rump. It's pretty hard to find these days.'

He laughed and wiggled the piece of anatomy she was eyeing. 'Don't go getting any ideas to sink your teeth into this just yet.'

'I wouldn't dream of it,' she said with a mischievous glint in her eyes, picking up the tongs and aiming a pinch his way. 'I'm very selective with my rump. It takes a lot of handling and careful weighing before I select the best piece.'

He sidestepped the tongs and made a grab for them in one swift movement. 'Glad to hear it. Now, if you don't mind, *this* rump is ready.' He gestured to the grill before filling a platter with two steaks, several prawn skewers and corn on the cob.

'I'm starving.' She reached for the plate, her hand brushing his, and for a split second when he raised his eyes to meet hers he read desire.

Or maybe it was a reflection of his rampant need mirrored there?

Rather than give in to the impulse to ditch the plate and haul her into his arms, he used every inch of willpower to step away and keep his response light.

'Good. I'm famous for my culinary skills.'

She followed him into the kitchen and the intensity of the previous moment dwindled away till he wondered if it had been a figment of his imagination.

'Is there anything you're not good at?' She placed the salad and herb bread on the table next to the mixed grill while he poured the merlot. 'Because, from where I'm sitting, you're almost too good to be true.'

He paused, surprised by her swift change in mood from playful to serious. In the past, he'd been labelled with the tag most guys hated, the dreaded 'nice', though the women he'd dated hadn't seemed to mind. In fact, he'd been complimented on his manners and the way he'd treated them in general. It hadn't been his fault those relationships had failed. Supposedly, nice guys always finished last, and the women he'd been involved with had seemed to reiterate the fact.

He smiled and raised his wine glass to her. 'Give me a few hours. I'm sure I'll think of something.'

She clinked glasses with him, her eyes glittering

in the muted light. 'My friends have labelled you Mr Perfect.'

'You've been talking about me with your friends?'

This was good. Very good. That meant she was more interested than she let on, though he wondered about the 'perfect' tag. No way could he live up to those expectations.

Despite their instant, intense attraction, she hardly knew him, so what had he done to deserve the accolade?

'I might've vaguely mentioned something to them, you being a new client and all.' She speared a prawn and waved her fork around as if her comment meant nothing. 'Though I wouldn't read too much into it.'

'And here I was thinking you might be falling for my charm.'

She chewed and swallowed before answering, a smile playing around the corners of her mouth. 'Sorry to disappoint. Maybe you need to brush up on your technique?'

He liked the switch back to playful and he fully intended to keep the mood light for the rest of the night.

'Oh, I fully intend to.' He reached across and ran a fingertip across her bottom lip, watching her eyes widen, the dark pools tempting enough for any man to lose himself in their depths. 'How do you think I'm doing so far?'

He could've sworn her lip trembled beneath his light touch before she leaned back slightly and broke the contact. 'Needs some work but you've got potential.'

'Thanks. That's all the encouragement I need.'

He stared at her over his wine glass, trying to gauge her reaction to his comment. He'd made his intentions more than clear over the course of the day, and if she opted out now he'd be disappointed.

She reached over and lightly tapped his glass. 'Good luck, Doc. With me, you're going to need it.'

'Sounds like a challenge.'

She laughed, a light-hearted sound that warmed his heart. It had been too long since he'd unwound in the company of a beautiful woman, especially one who sparked his interest on many levels. 'Why do all men get that gleam in their eye at the thought of a challenge?'

'Because it brings out our competitive side.'

She rolled her eyes. 'Men!'

Enjoying their teasing, he decided to push his luck. 'Speaking of my Y chromosome, when am I going to see you in a bikini? After all, we're at one of the best beaches in the world, and members of the weaker sex such as me look forward to seeing the latest in surf fashion.'

And, just like that, the shutters descended over her eyes, cloaking them in a haze of emotion he could only label as disappointment.

'Dream on.' Though the corners of her mouth tilted up in a tight smile, the action was far from a happy gesture.

Okay, so she wasn't big on bikinis. Maybe he'd try a different tack to lighten the moment. 'Hey, can't blame a guy for trying. With a body like yours, seems a shame not to show it off.'

If the shutters had descended seconds earlier, this time the blinds well and truly snapped shut. She shrugged and toyed with the napkin at the side of her plate. 'Sorry to disillusion you, but remember those old neck-to-knee swimsuits? They're skimpy compared to mine.'

She managed a short laugh but it didn't fool him. He'd made her uncomfortable and, once again, she had him confused. This Jekyll and Hyde thing she had going on was frustrating the hell out of him and putting a real dampener on his eagerness to get to know her better.

Keen to defuse the tension that suddenly enveloped them, he raised his wine glass to her. 'I've always stuck by the more is less theory, so I look forward to seeing it. Now, let's eat.'

However, as he passed her the salad he had the distinct impression that eating was the last activity she wanted to do and, for the second time in as many minutes, wondered what deep, dark secrets Keely Rhodes harboured.

Keely trailed her fingers over the book spines, reading the titles but not really absorbing them. If she'd been nervous earlier, it was nothing compared to now. Dinner had been a breeze, with Lachlan switching to small talk after their initial hiccup over his bikini joke and she'd soon relaxed.

However, she'd known it wouldn't last, and as the evening drew to a close the butterflies in her stomach took flight. Though he'd deposited her overnight bag in the spare room when they'd arrived at his beach house, she knew that didn't necessarily mean she would be sleeping in there.

She hadn't been this attracted to a man before, and though she continued focusing on work—apart from her earlier lapse into flirt mode while he barbecued— her mind kept drifting to fantasies of getting intimate in the bedroom.

He hadn't helped matters much, stripping out of that wetsuit back at the beach and asking her to hold his towel up as a shield from prying eyes as he changed. The only problem with that was *her* eyes had been the ones doing most of the prying! Though she'd done her best to avert her gaze, she was only human and couldn't help but take a peek.

And, boy, had it been worth it!

An expanse of tanned skin covered rippling muscles that belonged on an elite athlete rather than a psychologist who surfed part-time. And that butt...

She was sure the towel had slipped a notch as her hands shook while she checked out the doc's hidden talents.

'See anything that interests you?'

She jumped as he entered the lounge room, knocking half a dozen hardback novels off the shelf in the process.

Rather than rushing to her aid, as she'd expected him to do, he chuckled and sat down. 'I'd offer to help, but one concussion a week is more than enough for me.'

'Very funny.' She bent to pick up the books, wondering if she'd ever be cured of her clumsiness. The way he intruded on her thoughts constantly, she doubted it. 'Thanks for dinner, by the way. It was delicious.'

'No problem. Wait till you see what I've got for dessert.'

She almost upended the books a second time. So much for putting a dampener on her imagination. With his words, she conjured up an instant vivid image of strawberries, whipped cream and the two of them sharing dessert…in very inventive ways!

'I haven't really got a sweet tooth,' she said, aiming for nonchalant when she knew she could easily forgo the edible dessert in favour of something much more enticing—like him on a platter.

'Couldn't be weight-related.'

And, just like that, the cosy atmosphere shattered.

Thankful he couldn't see her face as she rearranged the shelf, she swallowed the lump of emotion that lodged in her throat, mentally kicking herself for believing a guy like Lachlan could be different.

Every man she'd ever known had been obsessed about looks and weight, often making jokes about 'fat chicks' who didn't care about their appearance, or chuckling over advertisements for weight loss centres. She'd learned to steel herself against their cruel judgements, despite the urge to smack them silly.

As for taking a swipe at her own eating habits, only one guy she'd casually dated had ever made that mistake—and she'd let him have it, after accidentally spilling her wine over his crotch.

Lachlan had made several remarks about her body since they'd met and, though he probably saw them as innocuous, she knew what they really were—a sign that he was just like the rest of the guys she'd ever known, hung-up over looks and little else. Not to mention a clear indication she shouldn't get involved, no matter how much her body kept telling her otherwise.

He didn't pick up on her stiffening or, if he did, he didn't let on. 'You don't need to worry about that, you look great. Trust me, you'll love this.'

His qualifier didn't help. What if she didn't *look great*? Would he even give her the time of day? She doubted it. No male had, not till she'd shed half her bodyweight and almost died in the process.

As for trust, she'd believed in it too many times to count and had been let down every time. People, especially men, were notorious for saying the T word and then doing their best to give you reasons to *mis*trust them.

*Lighten up. Before he takes his business and your chance at promotion elsewhere.*

Taking a steadying breath, she turned to face him. 'What is it?'

'Close your eyes and let me guide you to it.'

'This better be good,' she said, allowing him to guide her through the room and out the door. When in actual fact she felt like bolting through it and not looking back.

'Oh, it's better than good.'

His hands were lightly resting on her hips as he gently propelled her forwards, and her skin fairly sizzled where he touched her. Damn her hormones! One minute she thought he was an insensitive clod, the next she wanted to jump him. She needed to get a grip on her wayward emotions—and fast—before she got a grip on him.

'Just a few more steps... Okay, open your eyes.'

'How did you know?' She looked at the plate piled high with doughnuts of every description, from cinnamon-dusted to choc-iced, her mouth watering at the sight.

Okay, so he'd actually meant dessert when he'd said it. Then why did she feel like a child who had just been told that Santa Claus didn't exist?

He grinned and offered her the plate. 'I saw the way you were eyeing off my doughnut the other day. If I hadn't eaten half of it already, I reckon you would've snatched it out of my hand and gobbled it in one go.'

'Very observant.'

*If he only knew.* She hadn't just been staring at the

doughnut when he'd walked into her office, but at the way his lips had been dusted in sugar and cinnamon, shaken by how much she wanted to lick it off.

'I've heard the way to a woman's heart is through her stomach.' He demolished two doughnuts to her one and she chuckled at his genuine enjoyment. 'So, sweet tooth or not, dig in.'

Choosing to ignore his earlier jibe about weight for the sake of her job, she selected a choc-iced, silently vowing it would be her one and only. Though she could've quite happily eaten the whole plate, her weekly allocation would be blown. She'd have to attend a Pilates class every day of the week to keep in shape.

Though she'd come a long way from her overweight days, the scare she'd received after collapsing, and the resultant devastating news that she wouldn't bear children, acted as a constant reminder to nurture her body rather than abuse it.

These days she enjoyed every morsel of food that passed her lips, exercised regularly and accepted her body shape—three things she wished she'd done as a vulnerable teen.

'If you're trying to butter me up for something, you're going about it the right way.'

Wiping his hands on a dishcloth, he said, 'Why do you always suspect an ulterior motive?'

'Because men usually have one.' She pronounced

it like the fact she knew it to be, at least in her experience.

'I'm not like all men.'

Well, he'd got that right. 'Appearances can be deceiving.'

If anyone should know, she should.

'What you see is what you get with me.'

Her gaze flickered over him, taking in his relaxed posture, one leg crooked over the other, his hands braced at his back. He was propped against the sink, looking sinfully handsome in denim which hugged his hips and a black polo shirt that moulded his torso as if it had been made for him.

If what she saw was what she'd get, she'd be a lucky girl indeed.

'And what's that?'

Though she wasn't in the mood for word games, she had a feeling that the developing tension between them needed to be addressed before she did something crazy, like fling herself at him.

Or, worse yet, sleepwalk right into his bed.

'Apparently, I'm Mr Perfect.' He smiled, though she noticed the way he shifted, as if uncomfortable with the tag. 'Or so you tell me.'

She sighed, wishing she'd never told him that.

'I might've mentioned something along those lines in a moment of weakness, but don't hold me to it.'

He shrugged, drawing her attention to the breadth of his shoulders. 'Don't worry, I won't. Living up to a title like that would be hell.'

*No, hell would be taking a chance on a guy like you.*

Trying to ignore her racing pulse, she crossed the kitchen and stood in front of him, torn between wanting to melt into his arms or walking straight past him—and temptation—and out the back door.

'As much as I'm enjoying this conversation, I'm beat. I think I'll go to bed.'

She didn't move a muscle as he leaned towards her, her heart hammering against her ribs. Though she hadn't meant it as an invitation, she realised her declaration had sounded like one, and her body quivered with anticipation, every fibre alert to a possible incoming sensual assault.

'Pleasant dreams,' he murmured, brushing a soft, lingering kiss across her lips, a kiss that left her breathless and yearning.

However, before she could blink, he ran a hand lightly over her hair, cupped her cheek for an instant and walked away.

# CHAPTER SEVEN

*'Most men I know are like mascara. They run at
the first sign of emotion.'*
*Tahlia Moran, best friend and cynic.*

'How was the weekend?'

Keely plopped on the couch next to Tahlia and
hugged a cushion to her chest. 'Good.'

Tahlia quirked an eyebrow. 'And I thought Librans
were supposed to be well-balanced, eloquent individuals.'

'What can I say? He lived up to his perfect reputation.' Worse luck.

'*In* and *out* of the bedroom?' Tahlia leaned forward, her eyes gleaming at the promise of gossip.

'I can only vouch for outside of it.'

Her friend's eyes almost popped out of her head.
'You mean he didn't make a move?'

Keely shook her head, mentally kicking herself for
being disappointed.

'Let me get this straight. This guy goes to all the
trouble to get you out to his love-nest by the ocean,
practically strips naked in front of you, cooks you
dinner and then nothing?'

Keely reached for her wine and took a sip before

answering. 'Nice twist, but in actual fact it was his beach house, he had to change after surfing, we shared cooking duties and—'

'Nothing, right?'

Keely sighed and nodded. 'Yeah, nothing.'

'I don't get it.' Tahlia flicked her strawberry-streaked fringe out of her eyes and popped several chocolate-coated peanuts into her mouth before continuing. 'The guy oozes sex appeal, he definitely has the hots for you, you're keen on him and you're two consenting adults. You do the math!'

'By my calculations, I scored a big fat zero.'

Keely had relived that sequence in the kitchen after dinner a thousand times in her mind. She'd been torn at the time between wanting to shrug off her reservations and get physical with Lachlan and holding him at arm's length. He'd annoyed the heck out of her with his cracks about bikinis and watching her weight, yet when he'd followed up with a compliment she'd been putty in his hands again.

When she'd crossed the kitchen and told him she was going to bed it had almost been a challenge, and his reaction hadn't been what she'd expected.

A chaste goodnight kiss, albeit on the lips, hadn't satisfied her. Not by a long shot. And what had she done about it?

Nothing.

She'd muttered something about being exhausted and rushed out of the room before she—or he—could change their minds.

His behaviour puzzled her. Despite the vibes she kept getting from him, he hadn't laid a finger on her. The guys she'd dated in the past would've taken advantage of the situation in a second. However, Lachlan Brant was living up to his reputation as Mr Perfect more and more every day, a fact that wasn't good for her peace of mind.

'Are you sure he's not gay?'

Keely glared at Tahlia. 'What do you think?'

An impish grin spread across her friend's face. 'Nah.' She dipped into the bowl again, managing to throw several nuts in the air, tilt her head back and catch them in her mouth. 'So, where to from here?'

Keely laughed. 'Nice to see our Director of Sales hasn't lost her touch. Where do you learn those tricks anyway? Another one of your courses?'

As if her friend wasn't busy enough, she also frequented business courses in her spare time, always pushing herself in all facets of her life, as if making up for a lack of something.

Tahlia sniffed and repeated the performance, this time managing to capture two peanuts in her mouth at once. 'They don't teach you this in Business Etiquette 101.'

'Does the college run courses in How To Read Men 101? And, if so, where do I sign up?'

Tahlia munched on the peanuts for a moment, her brow furrowed. 'Maybe he thinks you're not all that keen. After all, you've been sending him mixed messages.'

'Flirting is one thing, sleeping with him another. Besides, I thought he had a right to know up front so there'd be no misunderstandings later.'

'But I thought you wanted more?'

'Yes…no…I don't know! Stop confusing me!'

Tahlia chuckled. 'I think you're doing enough of that for the both of us. Why don't you just go for it? Don't forget, that's what your horoscope said.'

'They're called that for a reason. In my case, it's a horror-scope.'

'Don't mess with the stars.'

'Don't mess with my head.'

'Hey, that's the Doc's job, not mine.'

Keely stood and crossed the room, staring out at the stunning bay view. She loved watching the world go by from her sixth-floor apartment, particularly at dusk when the water took on a mauve hue.

Tahlia was right. She should stop procrastinating and go for it with Lachlan. What did she have to lose? It wasn't as if she was expecting happily-ever-after or anything remotely like it. They could date, have fun, and make the most of every day as people her age should be doing.

Why did she need to constantly overanalyse every situation?

*Because you're in deeper than you think.*

Telling her voice of reason to shut up, she turned back to Tahlia.

'Thanks for the advice, Dear Abby. Now, how

about we get down to the business of planning Em's surprise party?'

Tahlia scrutinised her for a moment before shrugging her shoulders. 'Nice change of topic. I'll buy it.' She picked up her pocket organiser and started flipping pages. 'I've booked Sammy's, organised the finger food with Andy, and drinks will be buy-your-own over the bar. How is the guest list coming along?'

'All done, though she's going to be pretty bummed that Harry isn't going to be there.'

'Time she got over him. Who pines after their first love for that long anyway? Men are all the same; they just have different faces so that we can tell them apart.'

Keely chuckled at her friend's cynicism. Though Tahlia had men falling at her feet, she seemed oblivious, hell-bent on conquering the world rather than the male species. Despite the way she ignored them, they still flocked.

'I think it's romantic. And, from the photos I've seen of the guy, can you blame her?'

'Point taken. What about a present?'

Keely picked up a magazine from the coffee table and flipped it open. 'I know this is kitschy, but what do you think?'

Tahlia took one look at the page and almost fell off the couch laughing. 'A Barry Manilow figurine? You've got to be joking!'

Keely joined in the laughter. 'But she loves the

guy almost as much as Harry!' She looked at the picture of pint-sized Barry and cracked up again. 'I think he's kinda cute.'

'And I think you're kinda crazy. Besides, I have a better idea. What about that toe ring she was eyeing off in the jeweller's window the other day?'

'The one with her star sign on it?'

Tahlia nodded. 'I think our Miss Conservative is going through a rash patch at the moment. She's never worn a toe ring in her life.'

Keely clicked her fingers and practically bounced around the room in her enthusiasm. 'Great idea. She's definitely after a change of image, so we can also do a makeover. Clothes, make-up, hair, the works!'

Tahlia's eyes fairly gleamed. 'Now you're talking. We can—'

The loud peal of the security buzzer stopped her mid-sentence and Keely glanced at her watch, wondering who her visitor could be. She rarely had company on a Monday night, apart from one of the girls, and the only reason they popped in so early in the week was usually to discuss some man problem from the weekend before.

She pressed the intercom button and said, 'Who is it?' And almost jumped back when Lachlan's deep tones filtered through the static speakers.

'Sorry to barge in on you like this, but do you have a minute?'

Keely turned to look at Tahlia, who leaped off the couch and gathered up her stuff in record time.

'Don't mind me, I'm outta here. Let the man up, for goodness' sake,' she mouthed while heading towards the door.

Keely glanced down at her candy-pink sweatpants and matching hood top and grimaced. 'Look at me. He can't see me like this. I look like fairy floss!'

Tahlia's wicked grin didn't reassure her. 'With any luck, he might eat you.' She gave her a saucy wave and sauntered towards the door. 'And I want details. Don't worry about buzzing him up. I'll let him in on my way out. Later.'

Keely groaned and shooed her away and, as Tahlia left, she rushed around the room frantically trying to clean up. Housework wasn't one of her strong suits, and as she'd been away for the weekend she hadn't had time to devote her scant hour to the usual once-over.

Resisting the urge to shove everything under her couch, she settled for making a few neat piles of magazines and clearing away the remnants of the girlie feast Tahlia had been devouring—wine, pretzels and chocolate-coated peanuts—just in time for Lachlan's knock at the door.

Smoothing back the wisps of hair escaping from her ponytail, and biting her bottom lip for a bit of colour, she opened the door. 'Hi. What brings you by?'

His gaze flicked over her and, rather than seeing

distaste, she read approval in the way his eyes lit up. However, it didn't appease her. She knew she looked a fright and wondered what he was playing at pretending otherwise.

'Sorry to drop by unannounced, but I'm going away for a few days on business and thought you might like this info.'

Her heart sank at his revelation. Just when she'd decided to take the plunge and see where all this tension between them was leading, he had to go away?

'Where are you going?'

He smiled, the simple action illuminating his face and speeding up her heart-rate in a second.

'I'll make you a deal. If you ask me in, I'll tell you.'

'Oops, sorry.' She stepped back, wondering why her manners deserted her whenever he set foot on her doorstep. It probably had something to do with the way he looked, and sounded, and smelt, but that was no excuse.

'Did I catch you in the middle of something?'

She closed the door behind him and resisted the urge to lean against it and sigh. He looked amazing in a dark grey suit, white shirt and burgundy tie— every ounce the consummate professional—and she looked like fairy floss! Not fair.

Smiling, she strolled across the room as if he popped in to see her every day of the week—she wished—and indicated he take a seat before plopping down into one herself. 'No, not really. Tahlia and I were just planning a surprise party for a friend.'

'Was Tahlia the stunning woman who let me in?'

A shaft of jealousy pierced her gut. Okay, so it was true, but did he have to notice that Tahlia's tall, slim figure could grace the cover of a magazine?

She nodded and wished she hadn't removed her make-up and changed when she'd got home. Tahlia had come straight from work and still looked a million dollars in her red power suit, with not a hair out of place at the end of the day.

'Tahlia is Director of Sales at WWW Designs. We've been friends for ages.'

He looked suitably impressed. 'Must be a rule at your workplace to only employ beautiful women.' He paused and allowed his glance to slide over her, very slowly, from head to foot. 'I like your casual look, by the way.'

She tried to detect a hint of sarcasm and came up lacking. He thought she was beautiful? Looking like *this*? Now she knew for sure. The Doc needed *his* head examined!

'Wish I could get out of these clothes,' he said, sticking a finger between his collar and tie in an attempt to loosen it.

*You can.*

She stared at him for a long silent moment before swallowing those two little words and turning away.

'Would you like a drink?'

'I'd kill for a coffee,' he said, following her into the kitchen. 'So, whose birthday party is it?'

'I'll trade you. You tell me where you're going—' *and why you're really here*, she thought '—and I'll tell you about the party.'

He leaned against the benchtop as she switched on the percolator and she wished he wouldn't look so at home in her apartment. It would make it hard to forget him when the assignment finished. And even harder if they started something that didn't involve work. She wouldn't be able to stand it when the inevitable split came—and it would. No matter how close they got, how well they clicked, he'd bolt like the rest the minute he learned the truth.

'Fair enough. The TV station hosting my new show is sending me to Sydney for a couple of days to check out something similar they screen up there.'

'Sounds interesting.' She poured coffee and added milk and two sugars to his, thinking how strange to find a man with a similar sweet tooth to hers, even if she'd told him otherwise. However, she added an artificial sweetener to hers, forgoing her passion for sweetness in exchange for zero calories.

While she had her head stuck in the cupboard, looking for some chocolate biscuits for him, he said, 'So what's the deal with the party? Is it some old boyfriend you don't want to talk about?'

She lifted her head too quickly and clunked it on the shelf above, cursing silently. There, that had to be another fault; he sounded jealous. Though, in a way, she should be flattered rather than annoyed.

'The party's for Emma, another friend I work with. And, as for not wanting to talk about boyfriends, that's true. I'm not one to kiss and tell.'

To his credit, he let that last comment go. She'd said it as some weird sort of challenge, almost daring him to ask about her previous relationships, though for the life of her she couldn't figure out why.

'That's good to know.' He took a sip of coffee before placing the mug on the counter. 'I like to keep my business private.'

*Huh?* Had he just said what she thought he'd said?

Rather than taking the easy way out and laughing off his comment, she pounced. 'Are you implying that you'd like to be my boyfriend?'

He fixed her with a stare that bored straight down to her soul, as if trying to probe into her innermost feelings. 'I'm not implying anything; I'm stating a fact.'

She hadn't moved since he'd dropped his little bombshell, her feet rooted to the spot, and he crossed the kitchen in a second.

'Pretty confident, aren't you?' She tilted her head up to meet his gaze, her pulse tripping as his eyes darkened to midnight.

'I call it how it is.'

A little demon lodged in her mind and prodded her with its pitchfork, urging her to provoke him further.

'And how's that?'

'You, me, dating. Seems straightforward to me.'

She didn't resist as he lowered his head towards her with infinite slowness and, with a sigh, closed her eyes. She'd been waiting for this, hoping for it, since that first time in her office when she'd been sure he wanted to kiss her. And if she'd thought the brief, gentle peck he'd delivered at the beach house at the weekend had been good, it wasn't a patch on this.

The minute his lips touched hers, it felt as if a match had been touched to a bonfire and whoosh! They both went up in flames.

Heat sizzled between them as she plastered her body against his, her hands delving into his hair in an effort to pull his head closer. He didn't disappoint, moulding her to his body with hands that wandered everywhere with skilled precision, stroking her till she gasped out loud.

Angling his head, he slid his mouth across hers in an erotic fusion, leaving her breathless. She melded into him, forgetting every last rational reason why she shouldn't be doing this.

His arms tightened around her and she felt his hard chest muscles tense beneath her hands. The fact he must work out was a fleeting thought. He felt so good, tasted so good, that she didn't want this moment to end, ever.

'Wow,' she murmured as his mouth left hers to

trail hot, open-mouthed kisses to her neck and back up again.

A shudder rippled through her as his hand slipped under her top and cupped her breast, sending fiery sparks of pleasure shooting to her core.

He broke the kiss to whisper against her mouth. 'What do you think of this dating thing so far?'

She clutched at the lapels of his jacket, knowing that if she let go she'd slide in a molten heap to the floor. 'Not bad.'

A smile tugged at the corners of his mouth, drawing her attention to those masterful lips and the fact that all he had to do was twitch them in her direction for desire to pool deep within.

'Mmm...maybe I need to brush up on my technique?'

Exhaling a shaky breath, she leaned her head against his chest. 'With me?'

Those two little words came out soft and needy, when she'd sworn never to be like that ever again.

She didn't *need* anyone. Needing only led to pain. And loss. And devastation.

He toyed with the strands of her ponytail while holding her close with his other arm.

'If you're volunteering for the job, it's all yours.'

*Say no!* A thousand reasons flashed through her foggy brain in a second.

*He's toying with you.*

*He'll bolt when he learns the truth.*

*He's too darn perfect and you'll never satisfy a*

*man like that. Once he sees the real you, he'll dump
you quicker than he can say love handles.*

Ignoring her fears, she lifted her head, looked him
in the eye and managed a mute nod in response.

Lachlan grinned as he left Keely's apartment building, more wired than he'd been in ages. He needed
to get home ASAP and go for a long bike ride, desperate to take the edge off his physical hunger for
the woman who tied him up in knots.

He'd hoped to steal a quick goodbye kiss before
heading interstate and it must be his lucky day, for
not only had his wish come true, it had blown his
mind in the process.

Attraction was one thing, off-the-scale rampant
need was another, and the minute his lips had
touched hers he'd known he wouldn't be satisfied till
they shared more than a kiss, their bodies entwined,
slaking a thirst that had him parched. For her.

However, in the midst of his fantasy, a tiny doubt
sprouted and took root. Keely had shown him a side
he didn't like, a side that reminded him too much of
his mother. She'd blown hot and cold too, all over
him one minute, walking out the next, and taking a
big part of his heart in the process.

As much as he wanted to explore the attraction
between him and Keely, he'd better watch out. He
didn't have room in his life for a fickle woman, no
matter how attractive.

In fact, if he were giving a caller advice, he'd

probably warn him to stay well clear of a woman who looked eager to devour him most of the time yet could change into the Ice Princess in a split second. And, though he'd admit to inadvertently arousing her anger by his throwaway attempts at humour, he knew her mood swings would get on his nerves after a while. A short while.

However, in this case, he had no intention of practising what he preached. He didn't want to stay clear of Keely; he wanted to get closer to her. The closer the better.

And if her mood pendulum swung once too often he'd walk away, heart intact.

# CHAPTER EIGHT

*'A good man is like quality coffee. He's rich, warm
and can keep you up all night long.'*
*Chrystal Jones, a woman who should know.*

'NO OFFENCE, but this idea for *Flirt* sucks!'

Keely looked at the sheet Tahlia handed her and
raised an eyebrow. 'But that's the image they're after. Bold, contemporary, out to make a statement.
They're a new magazine and they want something
totally different so I went all out.'

Tahlia merely shook her head in response and
handed the draft to Emma.

To her surprise, Emma's brow crinkled in a frown.
'You've done that all right,' she muttered, following
the flow chart with her index finger before coming
to an abrupt stop. 'Sorry, sweetie, I have to agree
with Tahlia. This idea will be impossible to animate,
let alone sell. And that's the bottom line here, making *Flirt* look as attractive as possible to the Heads.'

Emma placed her draft on the conference table between them and reached for a doughnut. 'And, unless
you want ours to roll, I suggest we come up with a
new design before the Rottie starts snapping at our
heels.'

Keely sighed, ignoring the doughnuts for once, and took a long sip of her Macchiato. 'Maybe I'm losing my touch?'

'More like losing your mind over you-know-who,' Tahlia muttered, cradling a steaming cappuccino in her hands.

Keely ignored the jibe. They were meeting to brainstorm ideas for *Flirt* magazine, their newest and biggest client, not dish the dirt on her status with Lachlan.

'When you said meet for a D&M, I assumed you meant the usual doughnuts and Macchiato, not the deep and meaningful conversation that often accompanies any one of us getting involved with a man.'

Though she needed to focus on her work—she could almost reach out and touch the promotion to Director of Graphic Design—the temptation to talk about Lachlan hovered in front of her. However, she knew that if the girls got her started she'd probably never stop.

'Do you want to talk about it?' Emma asked, the worried frown on her brow deepening. 'This stuff can wait.' She waved at the *Flirt* file as if it meant nothing, which they all knew wasn't true. If they ever lost an account like this one, it would probably mean their jobs would disappear quicker than a click of a mouse button on a delete key.

Keely glanced at Tahlia, knowing that out of the three of them she was the most driven. Her career meant everything to her, and if they veered from work during these regular meetings she would pull them back into line.

Today, Tahlia threw both hands in the air. 'What the hell? I'm up for all the gruesome details if you are.'

Keely placed her cup on the table, leaned back and folded her arms. 'Well, there isn't a lot to tell. He's a man, I'm a woman, and we're dating.'

'You're *what*?' Emma screeched, and grabbed her arm. 'When did all this happen? How did it happen? How far have you gone? What—?'

'Whoa! One question at a time, Em.' Tahlia leaned forward like a co-conspirator. 'Did you do the deed yet?'

Keely laughed and made a zipping action over her lips.

'Your lips are sealed, huh?'

She nodded at Tahlia, a smirk spreading across her face at the expression on Emma's.

'Now see what you've done,' Emma said to Tahlia. 'Ask one crass question like that and she clams up. Now what are we going to do?'

Tahlia winked at Emma. 'We could always go directly to the source and ask him. I'm sure Lachlan would love a phone call to his talkback show, asking about his latest love.'

'You wouldn't!' Keely burst out, knowing her friends were joking and enjoying it.

After her lonely teenage years, she'd thanked her lucky stars when she'd met Emma and Tahlia and for the instant bond that had sprung up between them. She valued their friendship more with each passing day and looked forward to their teasing as much as their kooky sense of humour and their loyalty.

Emma nodded. 'Yes, we would. Unless you give us some small titbit of gossip so we can live our lives vicariously through you.'

'Fine.' Keely took a moment to refill her cup from the coffee machine before responding. 'We're going away this weekend to Hepburn Springs for a little R and R. He's away on business in Sydney till then so in a way, it's our first official date.'

Tahlia rolled her eyes. 'Yeah, right. As if you haven't been dating for the last week anyway.'

Keely glanced at Emma, expecting her friend to say something. To her surprise, Emma chewed on her pen, a slight frown creasing her brow.

'What's up, Em?' Keely had enough doubts swirling through her head without her friends joining in. If something was bothering Em, the romantic dreamer of the three of them, it had to be serious.

'You really like this guy, don't you?'

Keely nodded, still a little stunned herself at the swiftness of the whole thing. Lachlan had entered her life just over a week ago and swept her off her feet. She never dropped her guard that quickly, though with Mr Perfect bombarding her with his presence on a daily basis, what choice did she have?

Thankfully, this time she had no intention of letting her heart rule her head. She knew the score: date a gorgeous guy, have some fun, don't get serious. No need for messy confessions about her past, no qualms about calling it quits. Simple.

Emma leaned forward and the frown deepened. 'I thought so. I've never seen you like this over a guy. Just don't get hurt, okay?'

Emma's concern puzzled her. She'd thought her friend would be doing cartwheels instead of doling out dire warnings.

'I really like him, Em, but I'm not about to do anything stupid.' *Like fall in love.*

No, this relationship would be light-hearted, casual, fun. They were dating, not on trial for potential marriage, and in that case her secret wouldn't even come into play.

'If you want my opinion, I think it's about time you lost it over a guy. All this realism garbage you spout gets a bit boring after a while.'

Keely smiled at Tahlia, knowing she could count on her for an honest update of the situation.

'On that note, I think we should get back to business. *Flirt* magazine should be our number one priority right now.'

At least during business hours.

She would have to make a conscious effort to concentrate on work for the rest of the week and banish the thought of her weekend away with Lachlan. Having him interstate and not popping up on her doorstep would certainly help, though her insomnia had taken a turn for the worse lately, and all she could think about while lying in bed at night was how far she was willing to take this dating business—and the possible repercussions—if the unthinkable happened.

By the way her emotions had been careening out of control around him she knew she had to tread carefully.

Dating Lachlan would be fine, loving him disastrous.

Though for the life of her she couldn't back away now. She deserved some happiness, however fleeting, and dating Lachlan promised to deliver in that department. In spades.

If anything, this weekend would be fun, and it had been too long since she'd had any with a man. Sure, her life as a city girl was rewarding, but she'd be lying if she didn't admit to a certain emptiness, a yearning for something more. And, right now, she knew Lachlan could fill that void—and how!

Keely jumped as Tahlia clicked her fingers in front of her face. 'Snap out of it, dating girl. Focus.'

Keely sent a sheepish smile her friends' way, banished thoughts of Lachlan from her mind and tried to do exactly that.

'You don't do things by halves, do you?' Keely glanced around the mud-brick cottage, admiring the antique furniture, the plump throw-cushions and a fireplace that just beckoned to be laid in front of. 'This place is beautiful.'

Lachlan deposited their overnight bags inside the door and looked up, his stare doing strange things to her insides even at a distance. 'You're beautiful.'

Though she knew his compliments were part of his charisma, as natural to him as breathing, a small part of her couldn't help but wish he truly meant them. Before a larger part told her to wake up! She looked in the mirror every morning, certain that her peculiar hazel eyes, brown hair and curvaceous body were nothing special. And far from beautiful.

She stood there, transfixed, as he crossed the room. Her brain—not to mention her body—had gone haywire the minute he'd picked her up from her apartment, his sizzling kiss a greeting she wouldn't forget in a hurry.

He'd said he'd missed her, but not half as much as she'd missed him. Was she insane? She'd known him less than two weeks. She'd recited 'don't fall in love…don't fall in love…' enough times over the last few days in the hope it would make a lasting impression. It hadn't, and she was at serious risk of losing her heart to this man.

If she hadn't lost it already.

'Nothing to say?' He tilted her chin up with his index finger while his thumb created havoc by brushing gently over her bottom lip. 'That would be a first.'

She stared into his eyes, knowing that whatever

happened between them she'd never forget that unique shade of blue. 'Are you suggesting I have a big mouth?'

His gaze dropped to her lips. 'There's nothing wrong with the size of it from where I'm standing. Nor the rest of you, for that matter.'

*Oh-oh.* There he went again. Another throwaway comment about her body. Sheesh, what was she thinking, losing her heart to a guy who was probably only interested in a svelte figure?

The minute his arms slipped around her she had her answer. She *wasn't* thinking. And it could prove her biggest downfall yet.

*Just shut up and kiss me*, she wanted to yell. Anything to distract from her doubts.

'Why don't you show me how much you missed me?' she said, sending him a coy smile designed to tempt.

'Again? There's no pleasing some women.'

She snuggled into him, inhaling his scent and allowing it to wash over her in welcome waves. She had to discover the soap he used and buy a cake of the stuff to keep next to her pillow. Maybe if she didn't have his body near her at night, his smell would be the next best thing to help her drift off to sleep?

'On the contrary, I'm very easy to please.'

He stroked her back, his hand burning a scorching trail through the thin fabric of her top. 'Tell me how.'

'Well, seeing as we're in Hepburn Springs, aka spa

country, why don't you start with drawing me a mineral bath, followed by a massage, topped off with a facial?' She accompanied her words by burying her face in his neck and nipping a light trail to his jaw.

'I hear the nearby spa facility offers all that and more.'

His hand stilled in its exploration of her back as she planted a row of tiny kisses along his jaw and upwards, till she reached the outer corner of his mouth.

'Who needs to go to a facility for all that pampering? I can offer you *all that and more* right here.'

He turned his head ever so slightly, fusing his lips to hers with the lightest touch.

The slow, burning kiss affected her more than any they'd shared before. As he deepened it, and she plastered her body against his, she wondered if this amazing toe-curling experience and its accompanying feelings indicated she'd already fallen for him, despite her vows to do anything but. Or could it just be plain old-fashioned lust?

'Stop thinking and just feel,' he murmured, caressing her body with skilled patience till she almost purred.

'Feeling is scary,' she said, arching against him despite herself, unable to stop the powerful surge of emotion that she didn't dare label love that drew her to him.

'I won't let you down.' He pulled away slightly,

cupped her cheek and stared into her eyes, and for one endless moment, she almost believed him.

'Can we slow things down a bit?' As the words left her mouth, she wanted to take them back.

She'd taken things slow her entire life, pulling away from people, sabotaging relationships with men, not willing to get too close. And where had it got her?

Alone. Unable to sleep at night. And still hoping for the perfect man to walk into her life and rescue her from all the insecurities that plagued her as a result of knowing the one thing she couldn't be in this lifetime—a mother.

Now the man of her dreams had come along and she was still balking, still holding back. Why? Wasn't he worth taking a risk for?

And in that moment she knew without a shadow of a doubt that she wouldn't think, analyse or hold back this weekend. She would 'go for it' as Tahlia had advised, and damn the consequences.

'Whatever you want.' He hugged her tightly and she relaxed, knowing that at least for the next two days everything would be all right.

Despite her fears, she did trust him. He seemed to be more intuitive than most men she'd known, so why shouldn't she take a chance and see where it led her?

'The girls were right. You are Mr Perfect.'

He smiled and planted a quick peck on the tip of her nose. 'In that case, I'd better start living up to my reputation. How about I draw you a mineral bath first and organise that massage you crave?'

'Mmm…sounds like heaven,' she said, knowing the only thing she really craved right now was him, but too scared to let go of all her reservations at once.

He released her and she immediately felt cold, bereft. 'Why don't you get changed and I'll call you when the bath's ready?'

She touched his cheek briefly, hoping he could read the clear signal in her eyes, the one that said *I like you. A lot.*

'Thanks for inviting me this weekend. I'm really looking forward to it.'

'So am I.' He looked ready to drag her back into his arms and she didn't move, already recognising it as a haven she could easily get used to. Instead, he gave her a gentle tap on the bottom. 'Now go.'

She grabbed her bag and headed into the bedroom before the anticipation of sharing more than a kiss with Lachlan sent her sprawling. Or, better yet, breaking one of the priceless antiques in his friend's holiday home.

Now wasn't the time for clumsiness. She'd come to the decision that this weekend was about romance and she had every intention to enjoy it.

Lachlan glanced around the bathroom for the final time, hoping Keely would like it. He'd always thought candles and flowers were reserved for a dinner table, but Will, his friend who owned this place—and a regular Romeo with the ladies from all accounts—had insisted the way to make a woman feel special was to use stuff like that in the bathroom.

So he had and, though it wasn't his thing, he had to admit the room looked pretty amazing. He'd never done anything like this before, but then he'd never liked a woman this much before.

It had taken every ounce of his willpower not to drag Keely into his arms and never let go earlier. The expression in her eyes had almost begged him to, in stark contrast to her whispered words to take it slow.

Despite her sassy attitude she appeared nervous, and the last thing he wanted was to scare her away. She meant too much to him and, though he might not ever take the relationship past the dating stage, who said they couldn't date for months? Maybe years, if he was lucky?

Marriage wasn't for everyone, and he knew plenty of people who remained in partnerships without an official piece of paper their entire lives. Hell, he'd counselled more married couples than those who weren't, and even if he hadn't seen the devastation the institution could wreak first hand with his parents, he would've probably stayed away from it anyway.

However, that didn't mean he couldn't enjoy a woman's company in exclusivity and he had every intention of making the most of his time with Keely. If she let him.

He'd glimpsed the vulnerability in her eyes repeatedly, as if she wanted to trust him but couldn't, and, though they hadn't discussed it yet, he had a feeling there was more to it than a past boyfriend. She retreated inwards at times, to a place she wouldn't let anyone else into and, though he respected her privacy, he needed to discover the reason behind her occasional aloofness before it drove a wedge between them.

Thanks to his deceitful mother, he stuck to the old adage 'honesty is the best policy' with an almost obsessive intensity and, though it might be too early to pry into Keely's secrets, he needed to know the cause of that fearful expression in her eyes at times—and who, or what, had put it there—before they got in too deep. As for her strange withdrawal from him when he made the occasional joke, it hadn't happened for a few days now and he'd lowered his guard, liking her warm, spontaneous side more and more.

A soft knock at the door had him casting one last critical look around the bathroom before he opened it.

'I thought you might've fallen in,' she said, pulling the robe she wore tighter across her front.

He tried to concentrate on what she'd just said, he really did, but it proved impossible with her standing there in a pale blue cotton robe looking like a cross between a knowing temptress and Orphan Annie.

He'd never known a woman so full of contrasts—

one minute the savvy city girl, the next a defenceless waif who looked ready to bolt at the first sign of trouble.

Luckily, the only trouble she would encounter here would be if he couldn't control his raging libido. He felt like a teenager around her, a totally foreign feeling. He was usually a man in control, a man who prided himself on being so. Though right now, with Keely standing in front of him looking good enough to eat, he was having a damn hard time remembering it.

However, if she wanted to take things slow, he would, even if he died of lust in the process.

'No, just making sure everything was ready for you.' He opened the door wider and gestured her in. 'Come in.'

She stepped past him and he caught a faint waft of apples. She used a fruity shampoo, and when he'd been away in Sydney he'd found himself consuming apples by the basketful just so he could enjoy the smell of them and remind himself of her. Pathetic, really, but who could blame him? She'd got under his guard so quickly and so thoroughly his head spun.

He watched her mouth open slightly as she looked around, enjoying her reaction. Despite his feeling silly about the candles and flower petals, the appreciative gleam in her eyes vindicated his actions and made him feel ten feet tall.

'This is incredible,' she murmured, reaching out

to take hold of his hand. 'No one's ever done any-thing like this for me before. Thank you.'

He squeezed her hand before raising it to his lips and kissing it. 'Take your time in here. Enjoy.'

Keely stared at Lachlan, the muted light cast by countless candles illuminating his face in a sensual glow.

The trouble he'd gone to in here had blown her away: the candles, the scented bubble bath, the rose petals floating on the water's surface, the fluffy white bath sheet hanging on a towel warmer and the soft jazz playing in the background. The room almost drugged her with its ambience, yet she had to remain focused if she were to thank the man responsible properly.

'Lachlan, I…I—'

'Shh…I know.' He held a finger up to her lips, effectively removing the need for her stuttered thanks. 'See you when you get out.'

Tears sprang into her eyes as he shut the door and as she stepped out of her robe and sank into the bliss-ful warmth of the bath, she didn't know if they were tears of gratitude or—dared she admit it?—tears of a much deeper emotion she'd vowed to avoid.

# CHAPTER NINE

*'It's not the size of the wand that's important, it's the way the magician wields it.'*

*Chrystal, an expert on wands.*

KEELY had tried to switch off her thoughts as she soaked in the bath. She'd imagined floating on an endless blue ocean, sitting beside a tinkling waterfall and swimming with playful dolphins. However, her relaxation techniques had had the same effect as they usually did when she tried them at home to drop off to sleep: nothing.

Instead, every time she'd closed her eyes Lachlan's image had popped up in front of her—his smile, the way his eyes crinkled in the corners when he laughed, how his eyes glowed after he'd just kissed her. Endless images that flitted across her mind, reminding her of how much she wanted him.

*And how much she wanted to let go of her reservations and love him.*

Yes, she'd finally admitted it. Despite being a realist with both feet firmly planted on the ground, despite all her silent protestations, and despite the fact that falling for a man like Lachlan would only end

124

in heartache for them both, she was inches away from falling in love.

Women in love did stupid things. She'd seen it time and time again with her friends and office colleagues, not to mention first hand. Though, strangely enough, what she was about to do couldn't be termed stupid. In fact, the tension between Lachlan and her had been building towards this since they'd first met. If she believed half the cosmic stuff Tahlia was into, she would almost say it was fated.

Taking a deep breath and tying her robe together, she ventured out of the bathroom. This was it. No backing down, no chickening out. No doubts about what he'd think of her body and whether she'd turn him on or not.

She wanted him and was determined to show him exactly how much. And if he was half the man she thought he was, despite his occasional insensitive comments, he'd accept her just the way she was.

'Lachlan?'

The house seemed strangely silent. Dusk had fallen while she'd been soaking in the tub and no lights had been switched on yet.

'In here.' She heard a muffled reply and followed it into what she'd assumed was a third bedroom.

'What are you up to now…?' She trailed off as she opened the door and stepped into another fantasy.

'Thought you might like a massage after your bath,' he said, gesturing to the table set up in the middle of the room, covered in thick towels.

She stepped into the room, shaking her head in amazement. If she'd thought the bathroom had been impressive, it had nothing on this—a slow-burning fire, champagne on ice, lavender permeating the air from an oil-burner and soulful sax playing in the background. All in all, she could've spent a month in this room, as long as the man standing in the centre of it, with a proud grin on his handsome face, came with it.

'If you're trying to seduce me, you're doing a good job.' She smiled and crossed the room, standing on the opposite side of the massage table.

He shook his head. 'This isn't about seduction.'

'Then what's it about?' Her heart thudded as he walked around the table and traced her cheek with the back of a finger.

'I wanted to do something nice for you, to make you feel half as good as you've made me feel since I met you.'

'But I haven't done anything.' She shook her head slightly, wondering if the prolonged soak had fogged up her brain as well as the bathroom mirrors.

'You don't need to.' His hand dropped to her shoulder, where his fingers toyed with the collar of her robe, lightly skimming her heated skin beneath it. 'You've made me happy just by being you. I haven't dated in a while and have forgotten how special it can be with the right person.'

She stared at him, speechless. In all the years when

her self-esteem had taken a beating, where had a guy like this been?

Correction, where had *this* guy been?

She'd been through the wringer with her weight issues, the accompanying hang-ups, the brush with an eating disorder that had ruined her chance at having children and the subsequent ramifications on her relationships with men since. Not to mention the hours of counselling that had left her questioning her own belief system rather than helping her overcome her problems.

And here, now, with just a few words, he'd made her feel whole again.

She blinked back the tears that had sprung into her eyes and reached up to twine her arms around his neck. 'You know what I said earlier, about taking things slow?'

He slid his arms around her, the heat radiating off him warming her better than the slow-burning fire. 'Yeah?'

'I've changed my mind.'

And she set about showing him exactly how.

Keely floated into the office on Monday morning. She'd had the barest minimum of sleep for the entire weekend and didn't care. She'd never felt so alive, so animated, as if she could take on the world and still have enough energy left over to tackle the solar system.

She had a pile of work to get through this week

and, as she dumped her satchel and booted up her computer, all she could think about was Lachlan.

She would have to add one more criteria to her checklist for the perfect man: incredible lover.

If she'd thought his skill at kissing was impressive, it had nothing on his performance in the bedroom. And the lounge room. And the kitchen.

And if she'd thought massage was mainly used as a relaxation technique, she'd had to think again.

Scanning her e-mails quickly, she ignored the inter-office ones and opened Emma's.

To: *KeelyR@WWWDesigns.com*
From: *EmmaR@WWWDesigns.com*
Subject: D&M
Hi Sweetie,
Got time for a D&M in the conference room?
Need a few details for *Flirt* website (and a few from your weekend away?)
C U in 10?
Em


Keely grinned. She knew her friends would be dying to hear the gossip from her weekend away with Lachlan and, despite the urge to keep them guessing, she fired off a quick reply.

To: *EmmaR@WWWDesigns.com*
From: *KeelyR@WWWDesigns.com*
Subject: Only 10?

Em,

Surprised you can wait 10 minutes.

Ideas for *Flirt* website coming along nicely.

Will bring my revamped work.

Have doughnuts and Macchiato at the ready.

C U soon.

K

Gathering up the *Flirt* file, she heard two beeps from her PC. The first e-mail was from Tahlia, reiterating what Emma had said and wanting 'all the gory details', the next from Lucy.

To: *KeelyR@WWWDesigns.com*

From: *Lucy-PA@WWWDesigns.com*

Subject: PM sucks!

K,

Took your advice, asked Aidan out for coffee.

Put the PM quiz to the test and he bombed, big time.

Wolf in sheep's clothing doesn't come close to describing him. How about ravenous wolf who devours his prey?

Dating is the pits.

How many men does it take to screw in a lightbulb?

Three: one creep to screw in the bulb and two to listen to him brag about the screwing part. That sums up Aidan—Yeuk!

Luce (reformed dater)

Aidan a sleaze? Keely shook her head, hoping her lousy judgement in men didn't extend to all facets of life. She could've sworn Aidan seemed like a nice guy, though appearances weren't everything.

Feeling more than a tad responsible for urging Lucy to ask Aidan out, she typed a quick reply.

To: *Lucy-PA@WWWDesigns.com*
From: *KeelyR@WWWDesigns.com*
Subject: Forgetaboutit!
Luce,
Sorry Aidan the Ass turned out to be just that.
The solution? Get back out there. Your PM could be just around the corner.
Drinks, this Friday after work. Be there.
Let the search recommence…
K

Hoping that Lucy wasn't too devastated about the Aidan fiasco, Keely headed out of her office, ready to face the music with her friends.

Several hours later, Keely sat in front of her PC and brought up the newest account that had just landed in her lap. *Bountiful Babes* promised to be a one-stop website for parents who needed the low-down on the joys of having children. Initially, she'd been reluctant to take it on—the fact that she loved kids and couldn't have any rubbed in her face wasn't good—

but with the Rottie breathing down her neck she'd had no choice.

Besides, she'd sensed something else behind the Rottie's urgency, almost as if they needed these new accounts to survive. Which was silly really, considering WWW Designs was one of the largest firms of its kind in the country.

However, she'd never juggled three prestigious accounts at once before, and this, plus the Brant assignment, added to her suspicions that something wasn't quite right. The Rottie had been snapping at everyone's heels for the last few weeks, raving on about deadlines and efficiency, and though she'd held her tongue because of the promotion she coveted, Keely had almost told her to shove it several times.

She'd managed to placate the Rottie with a pat on the head—figuratively speaking—and news that her assignment with Lachlan was proceeding extremely well. She'd just left out the part where her shadowing him had turned from business to pleasure.

As the preliminary work she'd done for the site flashed across the screen, she swallowed the lump of emotion that inevitably rose when she saw anything to do with babies. The motif she'd designed as a border for the web page—a chubby, chuckling baby in various poses—brought a smile to her face. From his ten perfect fingers and toes to his rosy cheeks and dimpled skin, he was adorable, and a stark reminder of what she could never have.

Sighing, she made an angry swipe at a tear escaping from the corner of her eye and turned away as someone knocked on her door.

She sat up straighter and fixed a smile on her face. Just her luck for the Rottie to come bounding in here and catch her sniffling. 'Come in.'

'How's my favourite graphic designer?' Lachlan strolled into the room and handed her a bag. 'I come bearing gifts. Thought you could use something to boost your energy levels.'

She opened the bag and inhaled deeply, the seductive aroma of fresh cinnamon doughnuts making her salivate, before casting him a coy look from beneath her lashes. 'I'm fine and there's nothing wrong with my energy levels. In fact, I haven't been this *energised* in ages.'

He laughed and chose one of the doughnuts from the bag she proffered. 'Glad to hear it.' He rolled his neck around as if trying to work out a kink. 'I'm in dire need of another *massage*.'

Heat crept into her cheeks at his emphasis on the word 'massage'. She'd done all that and more to him on the weekend away, displaying a brazen side she hadn't known existed.

As Tahlia had laughingly pointed out after she'd given the girls a very brief version of events, she was working in the right place: WWW Designs could stand for Wickedly Wanton Woman or Wonderful Wowsing Witch. Both labels seemed appropriate at this stage!

She interlocked fingers and stretched forward, as if limbering up. 'For you, any time.'

As desire arced between them and he crouched down beside her chair, she placed both hands on his chest and held him back. 'However, right now I need to do some work.'

He captured her hands and held them against his chest till she itched to slide her fingers between the buttons of his ivory business shirt and caress the firm skin underneath.

'I thought my website was nearly finished?'

She nodded, trying to think 'work' while this close to the man who had rocked her world repeatedly over the weekend. 'It is.'

'So what's this you're working on?'

He peered over her shoulder, ignoring her muttered, 'A client's work is confidential', his face breaking into a huge smile.

'That's one cute baby,' he said, his eyes glowing with a tenderness she'd never seen before.

She pulled away and swivelled her chair towards the screen, rattled by his reaction.

'You like kids?' she asked, trying to instil the right amount of casualness into her voice while hanging on his answer.

'What's not to like? They're amazing, taking over your life and wreaking more devastation than a cyclone. And I wouldn't have it any other way. I helped raise my younger brothers and sisters and, though challenging, it was the most rewarding thing I've ever done.'

His words drove tiny daggers of pain into her heart, opening up wounds she'd thought healed. She had to ask the next question, knowing his answer would seal the fate of their relationship, one way or the other.

'Do you want kids of your own?'

'Absolutely. If the right woman came along, I reckon I'd like at least half a dozen of the little tykes.'

And, just like that, reality crashed in, leaving Keely struggling for air.

She'd known that dating Lachlan could prove disastrous but she'd gone ahead and done it anyway. Despite her feeble protestations, he was business; she'd fallen for him, and labelling their relationship 'dating' had been a lie on her part.

She loved him, had probably loved him before she knew what had hit her, and therefore had ignored every warning that she shouldn't get in too deep. When relationships went too far, certain expectations came into play, and now she'd heard it for herself.

He wanted the one thing she could never give him.

And it would ruin them in the end.

Struggling to keep her voice steady, she said, 'Why settle for half a dozen?' She managed a brittle laugh before shuffling the paperwork on her desk. 'Now, it's nice of you to drop by, but I really have to get back to this.'

He frowned and stood up. 'Is something wrong?'

She shook her head and tried not to blurt out *Everything is wrong.*

'No, just the usual jitters that deadlines bring.' She looked away, only to be confronted by the computer screen and the evidence of what she couldn't give him, the pain ravaging her anew. 'Raquel wants this done ASAP.'

He didn't budge. 'Are you sure this is about work?'

She had to meet his gaze, if only to convince him that she needed to be left alone before she burst into tears. 'Of course.'

His direct gaze bored into hers, as if trying to see into the windows of her soul and read the secrets there. For now, she sure hoped the shutters were down.

'I'll leave you to it, then. Call me when you have a minute?'

She nodded and faked a breezy wave as she focused on the screen again, hoping he'd been fooled.

By the dubious look he cast her on the way out, she doubted it.

Lachlan slipped the headphones off and leaned back, grateful for the four-minute break a song from some boy band offered. He needed time to think and hadn't had much opportunity lately, what with the new TV show, the publicity demands and continuing with his radio talkback show, which had reached the number one ratings spot over the last few weeks.

Professionally, he had the world at his feet. Then why did he feel like a tightrope walker teetering on the brink of a big fall?

He rubbed his eyes and took a sip of the disgusting brew the station labelled coffee, knowing exactly why he felt so out of control these days.

Keely.

He'd thought he'd been dating the woman of his dreams. So how had their relationship turned into a nightmare?

Ever since their weekend in Hepburn Springs, which had been incredible, she'd withdrawn from him slowly but surely. Back then, she'd reciprocated his passion and they'd connected on many levels, so what had gone wrong?

She'd cited work pressures as being the cause of their sporadic contact, but he knew better. The secrets Keely harboured seemed to grow bigger with every passing day. He'd glimpsed sadness tinged with something more akin to despondency in her eyes on the few occasions they'd caught up, and despite gentle prodding she hadn't opened up.

Either that or she was snapping his head off for the smallest thing, and he'd had a gutful. It didn't take a genius to figure out she had some self-esteem issues and he'd been careful not to make any references to her body since the first few outbursts which had put him on the outer. He'd been patient with her, yet she'd pushed him away at every opportunity anyway.

And it annoyed him. Hell, it had him so riled he could hardly think straight. Here he was, a psychologist at the top of his profession, offering help to thousands over the airwaves, yet he couldn't breach the emotional walls of the one person he wanted to.

He'd reached out to her repeatedly over the last ten weeks, persisting when he could've given up. He'd grown to like her a lot, and she made him happy like no woman ever had. However, she'd eroded his patience. Being stuck in a one-way relationship when the other person's interest had cooled wasn't his style. He'd seen what that did to a man firsthand with his dad and, dammit, he wouldn't wish that on his worst enemy, let alone himself.

Unfortunately, as hard as he tried not to compare Keely to his erratic mother, her behaviour drew frightening parallels that had him ready to call it quits.

Just yesterday she'd flared up over an innocent question he'd asked about how her websites for other clients were coming along, mentioning the cute work she'd done for that baby site. He'd been trying to show his interest in her career, she'd taken offence, and when he'd retaliated with a rather abrupt 'Calm down', she'd stormed out of the café, leaving him gobsmacked.

Another nasty similarity to his mother; she had run at the first sign of trouble. If an inconsequential spat that hinted at the rumbling volcano about to blow their relationship sky-high could make her walk, imagine what would happen if things got really serious between them. She'd flee quicker than he could say, 'It's over.'

When she'd run out of the café, he'd been ready to chase after her and end it right there and then, before an incoming call on his mobile from the producers of his new TV show had distracted him long enough to cool off.

'Lachlan, twenty seconds.'

He looked up at the station manager and nodded, reaching for the headphones.

He needed to focus on work for now, but come Friday night at her friend's party Keely owed him some answers. He'd tired of her games and was more than ready to pick up his bat and ball and head home. Alone.

Keely clutched her belly and groaned. 'This bout of food poisoning is lingering too long. That's the second time in the last few days I've been sick.'

Emma handed her a glass of water. 'Here, drink this. You'll feel better.'

Keely took several sips before her stomach rolled again and nausea washed over her in sickening waves.

'Oh-oh, here we go again.' She made a mad dash for the toilet, vowing to avoid Peking duck for ever.

She'd never been this sick and, added to her lethargy, it made her want to crawl into bed for a week. Work had been manic, explaining her tiredness, but she'd eaten the Chinese food days ago and should be over it by now.

Bracing herself for the meeting with Emma and Tahlia to discuss her final presentation for *Flirt*, she staggered back into the conference room and fell into the nearest chair.

'Feeling better?' Emma had refilled the glass with water and handed it to her.

Keely nodded, wondering if she could beg off the meeting and head home. However, the Rottie had insisted they present her with the work done on the magazine's website—like yesterday—so she'd been up till all hours putting the finishing touches on the design stuff and needed to run it by her colleagues before the presentation.

Emma reached over and squeezed her hand. 'It'll be over soon and then you can go home, okay?'

'Sure,' Keely said as her stomach somersaulted for an encore.

Tahlia breezed into the room at that moment, looking fabulous in a new trouser suit. 'I wouldn't sit in that chair if I was you.'

'Why?' If Keely hadn't already been a pale shade of green she would've turned it anyway. Her friend wasn't just dressed to impress, she had the perfect hair and make-up to match. Little wonder the Rottie rarely picked on Tahlia; her professional look would intimidate the scariest of bosses.

Tahlia sniggered as she grabbed a coffee and sat opposite. 'Because that's the preggers chair.'

'Huh?'

'Every woman who sits in that chair falls pregnant.' Tahlia counted the list off on her fingers. 'Nadia was the latest, then there was Shelby before her, Annie from Accounts, Maggie in Animation and Sue from Marketing.'

Tahlia paused, smug grin in place. 'So you see, it must be the chair. And, seeing as you're now engaging in activities that would make that chair a danger to you, I'd be very careful if I was you.'

Keely managed a weak laugh as her mind started jumping to all sorts of impossible conclusions.

'Leave her alone; she isn't feeling well.' Emma placed a jug of water in front of her before taking a seat.

'See? It's worked already.' Tahlia laughed at what Keely knew must be the bemused expression on her face.

Her friends didn't know about her past; she'd been too ashamed, and, though they would understand, she'd rather relegate that sad time in her life to past memories where they belonged.

Therefore, Tahlia had no idea that the one thing she teased her about could never happen. Then why did she keep thinking that there could be more to this bout of food poisoning?

She'd skipped a period but that was nothing new. Her periods had never been regular and she'd put it down to work stress. It had happened in the past, thanks to her erratic hormones. But now, combined with the other symptoms she'd been having, a tiny seed of hope had been planted in her brain.

Could the doctor have been wrong all those years ago?

Sure, Lachlan used protection, but that method had never been foolproof. Just ask Nadia, her immediate superior and career woman, who had sworn to never have kids. She'd threatened to blow up the local rubber factory that produced condoms when she'd first found out the news.

Despite her stomach continuing to dance the Macarena, Keely managed a small smile. If there was even the slightest chance she was pregnant, she wouldn't blow up the factory—she'd personally kiss each and every employee who worked there.

'What are you grinning at?' Tahlia asked, holding her hand out for the *Flirt* file.

'Nothing,' Keely said, trying to ignore the urge to leap out of her chair and rush to the nearest pharmacy to buy a pregnancy test.

Emma stared at Keely. She'd always been the more perceptive of her two friends and Keely knew that her confusion must show on her face, besides the fact that she'd gone from puking her guts up to grinning like a madwoman in less than a minute.

'Are we still on for drinks this Friday night?'

Keely met Tahlia's gaze for an instant before looking away. Otherwise she'd probably burst out laughing and give the game away. They'd planned Emma's surprise birthday party for the end of this week and had everything arranged. Now all they had to do was get her there.

'Well?' Emma looked at Tahlia, obviously giving up on Keely.

Tahlia nodded. 'Yep. Are you still interested in that makeover before your birthday next week?'

Emma wrinkled her nose. 'Don't mention the B word. This year I'm not interested in celebrating.'

'Is it the age thing? After all, twenty-four is ancient,' Tahlia teased, and though Emma laughed, Keely knew there was more to it than that.

With every year that passed Emma continued to pine for Harry Buchanan, and the fact that he wouldn't be around this year was probably the cause of her friend's reluctance to celebrate.

'I don't care what you say, you're getting that makeover on Thursday night.' Tahlia rubbed her hands together in glee. 'Leave everything to me.'

'What do you think?' Emma glanced across at Keely and she gave her a thumbs up.

'It's a great idea. A change is as good as a holiday, some wise person once said.' And, if that was the case, she'd be in for the equivalent of an around the world trip if her wild suspicions were confirmed.

'Okay,' Emma said, running her hands through her long blonde hair as if already ruing the fact that it would probably be the first to go. 'Now, can we get down to business?'

Keely nodded and clutched her stomach under the conference table, silently praying for a tiny miracle.

# CHAPTER TEN

*'My definition of a bachelor? A man who has missed the opportunity to make some poor woman miserable.'*
*Raquel Wilson, obviously single and not loving it.*

KEELY stared at the small plastic stick with two blue lines for the hundredth time that week, her reaction the same. Joy. Pure, unadulterated joy, that swept through her body and lifted her spirits to a place they'd never been before.

'I'm pregnant,' she whispered, when in fact she wanted to run up the stairs of her apartment building and shout it from the rooftop.

The doctor had confirmed it yesterday and she'd been floating ever since. She hadn't bothered asking how and why, when she'd been told this would never happen by another member of the esteemed medical profession all those years ago. Instead, she viewed this miracle as a gift and would treat it accordingly— she'd treasure, cherish and love the little human inside her with every fibre of her being.

And tonight she would share her news with Lachlan. Sure, he probably hadn't thought of starting a family this early, but she was confident he'd come around. After all, hadn't he said he wanted a half-dozen of the little cherubs? The only blight on her happiness was the memory of his words, *'if the right woman came along'*.

When he'd said that, she'd half-expected him to glance meaningfully at her, to smile that secretive smile he reserved especially for her, intimating that he'd already met the right woman—her. However, he hadn't done any of those things. Instead, he'd calmly announced that he'd want six kids *if the right woman came along*. Though it shouldn't come as any surprise, he obviously didn't think she fitted the bill.

She'd known it from the start, the fact that she'd never be good enough for a guy like him. And now, when the most amazing thing had happened, she had no idea if he'd be happy about it or not.

She'd been holding him at arm's length for weeks, ever since she'd heard his wish for children. What was the point of developing their relationship when she couldn't give him a family? The more he'd pushed, the more she'd begged off, citing work as an excuse.

He hadn't called for a few days, his silence a clear indication she'd almost succeeded in her plan. After going off the deep end at lunch earlier in the week and walking out on him, she knew the end was in sight. She'd been deliberately treating him badly, hoping he'd take matters out of her hands and end the relationship, leaving her to mend her broken heart in peace.

For the life of her, she couldn't fathom why he'd stuck around this long after the way she'd treated him. The more she gave him the brush-off, the more determined he seemed. Perhaps it was the psychologist in him, trying to figure her out? If that were the case he'd sure have his work cut out for him!

Thankfully, she could now stop behaving like an irrational cow—an irrational hormonal cow!—and hope that he hadn't given up on her.

Things would change, starting tonight. And, though she wasn't completely delusional, expecting a profession of undying love, she hoped that he'd be happy with her news and could hardly wait till after Emma's party to tell him. Though she would've preferred to tell him beforehand, he had to work and had said he'd meet her at Sammy's.

And, seeing as the father-to-be needed to hear the news first, she would just have to wait.

Placing the pregnancy test back in its plastic bag and into the top drawer of her medicine cabinet, she closed her eyes and sent a silent prayer heavenward that Lachlan would see this baby as she did, as a testament to their love and the beginning of a future together.

Keely waved to Emma and Tahlia as they strolled into Sammy's, before glancing over her shoulder into the room they'd hired and silencing everyone with a finger over her lips.

'She's coming,' someone hissed, followed by a tittering of giggles.

A slight frown creased Emma's brow as she reached the back. 'What are we doing hiding in this corner? Our usual spot is over—'

'Surprise!'

Keely stepped back as the chorus of voices sang out, enjoying the stunned expression on her friend's face.

'What the...?' Emma's head swivelled between Keely and Tahlia while people from work swarmed around her, everyone talking at once.

Keely leaned over and squeezed Emma's arm. 'Happy birthday, Em. We know how much you love surprises, so...surprise!'

Emma smiled, a dazed expression on her face. 'I can't believe you did this and I didn't twig. You're usually lousy with keeping secrets.'

Keely returned her smile and thought, *not any longer.* She could keep a secret and it was a doozy!

'Enjoy the night, sweetie. You deserve it. And you look fabulous, by the way.'

Emma patted her hair self-consciously. 'I like this bob, even if I do feel bald.'

Keely chuckled. 'It's not just the hair, it's the whole package. Your clothes, your make-up. Watch out, next you'll be moving out of home!'

Emma rolled her eyes. 'And not a moment too

soon. I'm twenty-four now. Time to grow up, don't you think?'

Keely nodded, knowing her friend wasn't the only one with growing up to do. She was going to be a mother—a sure-fire way to guarantee she grew up, fast.

'Your man's arrived.' Tahlia pointed towards the front bar and Keely eagerly turned, barely restraining the urge to run across the crowded room and fling herself into his arms.

However, she needn't have bothered. Lachlan had his arms full already. With Chrystal.

'Oh-oh, trouble in paradise,' Tahlia muttered.

Keely handed her the fruit cocktail she'd been drinking and said, 'Hold this.'

'Before she flings it at her,' Keely heard Emma add as she stalked away.

Lachlan looked up as she neared and had the audacity to grin sheepishly and shrug.

There was nothing sheepish about Chrystal's response and the predatory way her eyes glittered in the dim lighting. 'There you are, Keely. Look who I ran into. The doc was just seeing if I had something in my eye.'

Gritting her teeth and refraining from putting something in Chrystal's eye—like her finger—Keely said, 'You should be okay.' *After all, you're wearing enough mascara to shield them from a dust-storm.* 'Want me to take a look too?'

Chrystal shook her head—and her huge chest followed suit—though, thankfully, Lachlan had the sense not to look in that direction. If he had, there was no telling what she might've done. She'd never been the jealous type, though her hormones seemed to have kicked in with a vengeance, her temper spiking to irrational in a second.

'See you later, Lochie,' Chrystal purred, a triumphant smile on her face as she sashayed away.

'*Lochie?*' Keely stood in front of the man she loved, torn between wanting to kiss him and slap him. 'Well, isn't this cosy? You two progressed to nicknames already?'

A puzzled frown creased his brow. 'She's harmless.'

The little demon that put in a regular appearance in her mind prodded her with its pitchfork—hard. 'Yeah, as a tiger snake. What do you call her, *Lochie*?'

Rather than laughing off her jealousy, as she'd expected him to do, he folded his arms and glared. 'Don't.'

'Sorry?'

Though they hadn't seen each other since her childish display at the café, she'd taken his agreement to attend Em's party as an indication he was ready to forgive her. Obviously, she had been wrong.

He held up his hand as if staving her off. 'Don't

do the jealousy act. It would be hypocritical coming from you at the moment.'

She almost reeled back, shocked by his words. 'What's that supposed to mean?'

This had to be a joke, right? Some sort of payback for holding him at bay? He'd laugh any second now and say, *Fooled you*.

He didn't. 'You need to care to be jealous and I don't think you do. Care, that is.' He ran a hand through his hair, sending dark waves wayward. 'We need to talk.'

*Oh-oh*. She knew what those four little words meant. He talked, she listened, he walked, she crumbled. Nothing new in the scenario, just new players. Unfortunately, she seemed to have a starring role every time, with a different leading man to break her heart.

'About?'

'I'm tired of playing games. You've given me the cold shoulder for weeks now and, rather than be honest about wanting out, you hide your feelings along with the rest of your secrets.'

Icy dread stole through her veins. This didn't sound like a man who would welcome news of her pregnancy. This sounded like a man aiming to end their relationship, just as she'd suspected.

'If this is about our fight in the café, I'm—'

'That's only part of it.' He cut her off before she could apologise. Not that it would do any good. He had a determined glint in his eyes, as if he had his farewell speech already worked out. 'You're all over me one minute, barely speaking to me the next. I thought by coming here tonight we could see if there was any hope for us but I can see there isn't.'

Fury surged through her, replacing dread in an instant. 'And when did you figure this out? Before or after Chrystal thrust her enhancements in your face? Nothing like a killer body, is there? Pity mine didn't match up, what with you thinking I need to watch my weight and all.'

He stared at her as if she'd sprouted horns. Which was appropriate, considering the demon in her brain hadn't let up. 'I have a friend who can help you.'

'Help me?'

'Sort through the issues you have.'

Great. Rather than offering her his love, he thought she needed a shrink. And, worse, he wasn't volunteering for the job, which showed exactly where she stood with him.

'Never mind.' She shook her head, wondering how what should've been the happiest night of her life had turned into a disaster before it had even started.

'Look, I don't think—'

'No, you don't, do you? If you did, you'd accept it when I say I have work pressures and can't see you. You'd understand why I'd be jealous to see the office tart draped all over you.'

He shook his head, casting her a pitying glance.

'Maybe that's the first honest thing you've said to me. What about the rest?'

'The rest?' She gaped at him, wondering if she could blame the fog clouding her brain on hormones too.

'You've got secrets, Keely, starting with that phone call you made to my show a few months ago.'

'You know…' She trailed off, feeling a fool for not confiding in him earlier. She'd thought he would laugh it off, and maybe he would have if she'd told him herself. However, in the heat of the moment, her silence looked incriminating. What would he think about the rest?

He frowned, looking more foreboding than she'd ever seen him. 'I've known since the start. I remembered your voice straight away and thought it was pretty funny at the time. However, the closer we got, the more you clammed up. I saw the shadows in your eyes all those times you pushed me away and it made me wonder what else you were hiding and why you couldn't tell me about something so trivial.'

She almost reached out to him, then thought better of it. He didn't exactly look receptive at the moment, and if she didn't tell him the truth she could lose him.

'I wanted to tell you but would've been forced into dumping the rest on you and I didn't want to scare you off.'

She glimpsed a softening in his expression. 'Do I look like the type of guy to run?'

She shook her head and sighed, wishing she'd had the sense to do what he'd asked her at the start—to trust him. 'You're right; I do have issues. I thought I'd got past them, but I'm still oversensitive at times. That night I made the phone call to your show was the anniversary of a particularly difficult time in my life and I'd had a few drinks. When I heard you dishing out advice to that overweight teenager, something inside me snapped and I called up.'

She paused for a moment, wondering how far she should take her explanation. Not a muscle twitched on his face as he stared at her in stony silence, and in that instant she knew she would have to tell him everything or risk losing the love of her life.

'Her plight was too close to home. I was that teenager years ago, desperate for help and finding none. My parents didn't care, I didn't have any friends, and my psychologist spouted a whole lot of garbage when I needed help the most. That night on the radio you said something that triggered a reaction and the rest...' She spread her hands before him. 'Well, I guess you remember the stupid names I called you.'

'And you didn't tell me all this because you thought I'd run?' He didn't reach for her as she'd hoped. He didn't smile or touch her. Instead, he continued to stand there with his arms folded, looking unmoved, and the flicker of alarm that had shot through her when they'd first started talking turned into full-scale panic. 'What sort of a man do you take me for?'

Before she could answer, he said, 'Don't answer that. You've already made it perfectly clear.'

He picked up his jacket from a nearby barstool and shrugged into it. 'Look, I'm sorry for what you went through all those years ago, I really am. However, I asked for honesty at the start of this…whatever it is we were involved in…and I didn't get it.'

She felt the blood drain from her face at his use of the past tense 'were'. 'It's called a relationship.'

He shook his head. 'To you, maybe. To me, we were just dating.'

Pain lanced through her and she held a hand against her stomach in a purely reflex gesture, as if trying to protect their child from hearing its parents argue.

'So you weren't ever interested in anything long-term? What about all that stuff you said about having kids?'

She saw the hurtful truth in his eyes before he nodded. 'Dating is as far as it goes for me, as far as it ever would've gone. To bring kids into this world I'd have to be damn sure I could trust the mother of my children and, by the way all this has panned out, that woman isn't you.'

'I see.' Her words came out a whisper as her grip

around her belly tightened. However, before she could say anything else, his mobile phone rang.

Torn between wanting to walk away from the best thing that had ever happened to her and fling her news in his face to get a reaction out of him, she watched him pale and clench the phone against his ear.

She heard him say, 'When? Which hospital? I'll be there in fifteen minutes,' before hanging up and thrusting the phone back in his pocket.

She laid a hand on his arm without thinking. 'Is everything okay?'

He looked down at her hand, as if wondering what it was, before shrugging it off. 'I have to go. My dad has had a heart attack.'

'I'm so sorry,' she said, wanting to be by his side despite his callous words a few moments earlier. 'Would you like me to come with you?'

He fixed her with an icy stare. 'I don't think so. You haven't exactly been the most supportive girlfriend the last few months. What's changed now?'

This was her opportunity to tell him about the baby but she stalled, knowing it wasn't the right time. 'I'll tell you later.'

He shook his head and started to move away. 'I haven't got time for this and, as far as I'm concerned, there won't be a later. Let's just end it here and move on.'

In that instant her fickle hormones surged again,

jump-starting her brain into first gear along with her temper. 'Is that right? You think we were *just dating* and now we *just end it*?'

'Yeah.'

'What if I love you? And what if I said I was *pregnant*?'

If he'd been pale before, he positively blanched now. 'I'd say you'd go to any lengths to trap your idea of the perfect man and, just for the record, I'm not him.'

He practically ran out the door, leaving her standing there with tears streaming down her face and her hands clutched over her stomach, alone with her baby who would never know its father.

# CHAPTER ELEVEN

*'Lachlan isn't afraid of commitment. He's monogamously challenged.'*

*Emma, a supportive friend.*

LACHLAN rushed into his father's hospital room, expecting to see a sick, shaken man. To his surprise, Derek Brant sat up in bed, scowling at the various leads hooking him up to countless monitors.

'About time you got here. Look at me, trussed up like a turkey. Can't you do something about this?'

Lachlan exhaled, unaware he'd been holding his breath, as he entered his dad's room. He'd been expecting the worst, despite what the doctor and nurses had said, yet here his father was, sitting up and looking ready to unhook his shackles and escape.

He crossed the room and bent down to give his dad a hug. 'You've had a heart attack, you need to be monitored, so just leave those trusses alone, okay?'

His dad returned his embrace for all of two seconds before pulling away. 'What took you so long? I could've been dead and on a slab downstairs by the time you got here.'

Lachlan bit back a smile. His dad hadn't lost his

157

gruff manner and was obviously going to be fine. 'I was at a party and came as soon as I heard.'

His dad snorted. 'Off gallivanting with that pretty young thing of yours, eh?'

Lachlan had tried to block Keely from his mind as soon as he'd left the party, determined to concentrate on reaching his father. However, now that he'd seen his dad was okay, the full impact of what she'd said hit him with renewed force.

'She's not mine any more,' he said, wondering if anything she'd told him tonight had been the truth.

He'd seen the pain in her eyes when she'd discussed her weight problem and her empathy for his teenage caller, so he could safely assume she'd been honest about that. Besides, it explained her bizarre behaviour every time he mentioned anything remotely connected with body image.

But what was all that baloney about loving him after he'd ended it? Not to mention bringing up a possible pregnancy?

He shook his head, well acquainted with the lengths some women would go to to trap their man, his mother being a prime example.

'What happened?' His father fixed him with one of his infamous *don't think about fobbing me off, boy* looks.

'She reminded me of Mum,' he blurted out, before silently cursing himself for bringing up the one topic known to wind his father up, especially at a time like this. 'Fickle, unpredictable and totally incapable of maintaining an honest relationship.'

To his surprise, his father didn't swear and flush an angry crimson as he usually did when the subject of his ex-wife arose. Instead, he sighed and leaned back against a mound of pillows. 'I think we need to talk, son.'

Lachlan shook his head. 'I'm sorry I brought her up, Dad. This isn't the time. You need to concentrate on getting well, not getting worked up.'

His father stared at him with the familiar stubborn glint in his eyes. 'I'm fine,' he snapped, 'and you need to hear this.'

Lachlan sat back, knowing it was useless to argue when his father was like this. It would be easier to remain calm, hear him out and change the subject, quickly.

'Why do you say your young woman reminded you of your mother?'

Lachlan tried to ignore the pain he knew his explanation would resurrect. Despite his vow to never commit to a woman long-term, let alone think of marriage, that was exactly what he'd done within a month of dating Keely. He'd fallen in love with her, going as far as buying a house recently in the hope of convincing her that they could live happily ever after.

And what had she done? The closer he'd wanted to get, the more she had pushed him away with pathetic excuses and loaded silences. Even then he'd made allowances for her, had given her breathing space, yet it had all been for nothing. Tonight, when she'd done the whole jealousy routine that women had down pat, on top of her recent walk-out, something inside him had cracked and what she did or said didn't matter any more.

Okay, if he were completely honest, he'd gone to the party looking for an excuse to end it anyway. Picking that fight courtesy of her jealousy had made it all the easier. And, even as she'd spoken of telling him the truth, he'd seen the secrets behind her eyes. He couldn't live with a woman like that, couldn't trust her with the one thing he'd sheltered since his mum abandoned him all those years ago—his heart.

He could've predicted her protestation of love at the end. Most women would say anything to hold on to a man, even if it was a lost cause, but her words of a supposed pregnancy shocked him the most.

After his mother had left all those years ago, he'd overheard his aunt and father talking about how she'd trapped his father into marriage with her pregnancy. His aunt had said it was the worst thing a woman could do and his father hadn't disagreed.

'And what if I said I was pregnant?'

Keely's words, flung at him like barbs intended to wound, had brought back memories of his mother's treachery, and he wanted nothing to do with a woman like that. He'd get over her and never, ever, be duped again.

His father reached out and placed a gnarled hand on top of his. 'Tell me, son.'

'She blew hot and cold all the time, just like Mum. And when the going got tough she ran like Mum too. Then, after I'd ended it, she tried to hold on to me by saying she loved me and insinuating she could be pregnant, like Mum trapped you.'

'Ah, hell,' his dad muttered and, before Lachlan could stand up, tuck the bedclothes around him and bring an end to this conversation, his dad tightened his grip.

'Your mother didn't trap me, son. It was the other way around.'

'What?' Lachlan leaned closer, not sure if he'd heard the almost-whispered words correctly.

'I'm not proud of what I did but it happened. And, though I should regret it, I don't, because I look at you kids and thank God every day that I did it.'

Lachlan shook his head, wondering how much morphine his father had in his system. 'You're talking in riddles, Dad.'

'When your mother told me she was pregnant I forced her into marriage, even though she said she didn't love me. She was happy for a while after you came along but I could see that her heart just wasn't in the marriage. So, to bind her closer to me, I insisted we have more kids.'

His father rubbed his free hand over his eyes, as if trying to wipe away a host of unpleasant memories. 'I think she did it out of pity for me. The more I tried to make her love me, the further she pulled away. That's why she acted like she did most of the time. I drove her away, son, with my obsession for her. When she left, it was as much my fault as hers.'

Lachlan sat back, stunned, grasping for the right words to say and coming up empty.

'So, you see, your young woman…Keely, isn't it?…she's nothing like your mother. If she said she loves you you hold on to her tightly and never let go. Having the genuine love of a good woman would be the greatest gift a man could ever have.'

Spent, his father finally leaned back on his pillows. 'Now, leave an old man to rest in peace, figuratively speaking, hopefully, while you convince Keely to take you back.'

Lachlan wanted to ask his father a thousand questions about the past but now wasn't the time. His dad was right. He had to win back the love of his life. Though, after what he'd put her through, he knew words or small peace offerings wouldn't cut it. He needed to make a grand statement and hope to God she'd forgive him.

Suddenly, he knew just the way to do it.

Keely had barely entered her office on Monday morning when Lucy pranced in, looking like a perky zebra in her black and white striped ensemble. She usually loved her assistant's funky taste in clothes, but not today. Even the sight of Lucy couldn't cheer her up.

'I'm the bearer of bad news.'

'So what's new?' Her whole life could be an advertisement for bad news, all except the little life growing inside her, of course.

'The Rottie just cornered me, saying that the TV execs producing Lachlan Brant's new show need to see his completed website. Today.'

Keely swallowed the lump that rose in her throat and blinked furiously, not willing to shed one more tear over her Mr Not-so-perfect. She'd done enough crying over the weekend to last her into the next century, but no more. He wasn't worth it.

Despite their goodbye, a small part of her had hoped he would contact her over the weekend, just to see if she was okay. Instead, her phone hadn't rung and the only visitors she'd had were Emma and Tahlia, plying her with cups of tea, tissues and doughnuts as they cursed all men in general.

And, by Lucy's careful expression as she mentioned Lachlan's name, she knew that the girls must've filled her in on the situation.

'It's not so bad,' Keely said, determined to put on a brave face, at least during office hours. 'The website is finished. When are they coming in?'

Lucy grimaced. 'They're not. They want you to go to them, some place in Albert Park.'

Keely sighed and wondered where she'd gone so wrong. Was she so horrible that Lachlan couldn't even bear to see her? Was that why he'd probably gone to the TV station and coerced them into viewing her work rather than checking it himself?

So much for love. So much for Mr Perfect.

The first thing she would do when she arrived home tonight was tear up that stupid checklist. And burn the rest of the collection.

'Fine, I'll do it. E-mail me the address. What time did they say?'

'Three o'clock.' Lucy paused on her way out and swung around to face her. 'Don't bother coming back to the office. I can handle things here.'

Keely leaned back and shook her head. 'You know, don't you?'

Lucy nodded. 'Yeah, Emma told me about the break-up. She said she didn't want me blundering around in here, putting my big foot in my mouth while I blathered on about Lach—' She clamped her hand over her mouth, her eyes wide.

Keely managed a shaky laugh. 'It's okay, you can say his name. You did before anyway.'

'But that was business,' Lucy garbled through her fingers before lowering her hand. 'Seeing as you brought him up, I just want to say that I'm here for you if you need anything. Like a voodoo doll of the guy, a few sharpened pins, a dartboard with his photo in the bull's-eye… Get my drift?'

'Thanks, Luce, but I'll be fine.'

Lucy sent her a sceptical look that read *Are you insane?* before waving and shutting the door behind her.

*I'll be fine.*

She'd hoped that by now, after repeating the words time and time again over the weekend, she would start to believe them.

Instead, they sounded as hollow and empty now as they had then.

*Just like your heart.*

Ignoring the pain that knifed into the organ that Lachlan had broken without trying, she looked down at her flat stomach and murmured, 'Looks like it's just you and me, kid.'

Clutching her satchel and laptop, Keely knocked on the door of the stately mansion. Nice place, if you could afford it. TV execs must earn a squillion to afford something this extravagant in the upmarket suburb of Albert Park.

She just hoped they liked her presentation so she could get this ordeal over as quickly as possible and erase the name Lachlan Brant from her memory banks for ever.

'It's open,' a muffled male voice shouted from somewhere out the back.

Shouldering her load, she opened the door and admired the polished oak floors in a hallway that stretched as far as the eye could see. She wandered in, surprised at the airy feel of the place. Some of these dignified old homes tended to be dark, dreary places but not this one. Personally, she preferred the contemporary feel of her trendy apartment, but this old place had a lot of charm.

As she looked up at the ornate ceiling and cornices, the hair on her nape prickled, the same way it usually did when one man was near.

'Hey, Keely.'

Her gaze drifted slowly downwards. She needed to confirm what she'd just heard wasn't an auditory hallucination.

'Thanks for coming.' Lachlan stood in a nearby doorway, looking every bit as good as she remembered. Black shirt, black jeans, with his hair mussed in that way that made her fingers itch to smooth it.

However, after the way he'd trampled over her heart, surely that itch in her fingers was to slap him rather than run them through his hair?

'What are you doing here?' The words came out sounding a lot calmer than she'd expected as she carefully placed her laptop and satchel on the ground, before she was prompted to do something crazy— like fling them at him Frisbee-style.

'I needed to see you.'

Her gaze darted to the door as she wondered how quickly she could escape. However, he was a smart man. He hadn't taken a step towards her, for if he had she would've been forced to flee, professionalism be damned. In the past, she might've stood her ground and fought for the man she loved, but not this time. She'd bared her soul to this guy and what had he done? Dismissed her like yesterday's news.

As she'd originally thought when they'd first met, she wasn't good enough for him. He'd made that patently obvious by saying she couldn't be the mother of his children. Well, she'd show him. She didn't need some uptight, pretentious psychologist to parent her child. She would do a fine job of raising her child on her own, without the input of a man who thought she didn't measure up.

Instilling the right amount of *I don't give a damn* into her voice, she said, 'Naturally, you'd want to see the finished product. If you'd show me to a table, I can boot up the laptop and you can take a look at your new website.'

'That's not what I meant.' He made the mistake of moving towards her then and she held up her hand to hold him off.

'I'm here for one reason only and that's business. If you want to discuss anything else, I'm not interested.'

'We need to talk.' He stopped two feet in front of her, two feet too close.

She could smell his soap, as if he'd recently showered, and it resurrected painful memories she'd rather forget—like the first time she'd got close enough to smell it, the way its scent had clung to his pillow the morning after they'd first made love and how she'd buried her face in that pillow, unable to get enough of him.

'That's becoming your catch-cry, isn't it?' She

shook her head. 'I think you've said enough. Now, the website?'

'Forget the damn website!' he muttered, reaching towards her.

She backed away, almost tripping in her haste, and he thrust his hands in his pockets instead, cursing softly.

'This isn't going to happen, Lachlan. Not now, not ever.'

To her amazement, he strode past her, locked the front door and pocketed the key.

She laughed, a bitter sound that sounded nothing like happiness. 'You think you can lock me away like Rapunzel? Well, I've got news for you, mister. This isn't a fairy tale and you sure as hell aren't Prince Charming.'

'You're right. I'm not Prince Charming, Mr Perfect or any other fictitious character you care to label me with. I'm not some dream man who won't put a foot wrong, who won't ever say or do the wrong thing.' He reached for her and grabbed her upper arms and she stood there, too surprised by his outburst to move.

'I'm just a normal guy who's so head over heels in love with you that he can't think straight, let alone say the words you want to hear.'

Her heart leapt at his words, before settling into misery again. His sudden turnaround had to be about the baby. He'd thought about it over the weekend and had decided that having a child of his own was worth putting up with her for, even if she wasn't good enough to be the mother of his children by choice.

As much as she loved him—and as much as this baby deserved a father—she wouldn't risk her heart again. He'd had his chance to love her for *her*, and he'd blown it. Big time.

Shaking her head, she blinked back tears. 'You'd do anything for this baby, wouldn't you?'

He dropped his arms, a stunned expression on his face. 'You really are pregnant?'

'Of course,' she snapped, wondering if his short-term memory was functioning. 'I already told you at the party, remember? Around the time you dumped me? Ring any bells?'

Confusion clouded his eyes as he stared at her. 'But I thought you were just posing a question.' His eyes narrowed, as if trying to remember her exact words. 'Didn't you say something like ''What if I said I was pregnant?'' That sounded like a big ''what if'' to me, not a declaration.'

'You're splitting hairs,' she said, trying not to agree with him. Perhaps she hadn't made it clear that night. Not that it would've made a difference. He'd walked away from her anyway. Worse, he'd accused her of using something like that to hold on to him, which showed exactly what he thought of her. 'Besides, what difference does it make? I opened up to you, you rejected me. End of story.'

However, she couldn't ignore one salient point. If

he hadn't known she'd been serious about the baby, why say he was in love with her now? What did he hope to gain?

He tilted her chin up and, despite her efforts to look away, her eyes were drawn back to his. 'This is the beginning for us, not the end.' He smiled and it lit up his entire face. 'We're really going to have a baby? That's incredible.'

She wouldn't be swayed by his tenderness or smooth words. The time for saying the right thing had passed and she'd be better off concentrating on building her own future rather than dwelling in the past.

'You blew it, and as far as I'm concerned there's no going back.'

*You hurt me*, she wanted to scream, but swallowed the words like she always had, preferring to bottle up her feelings and withdraw from those who cared rather than risk being let down.

It had happened to her repeatedly as a teenager, and she'd learned to be self-sufficient and not rely on the approval of others to get through life. Now Lachlan, the man she loved, had let her down at a time she needed him the most and she'd be damned if it happened again.

'Tell me how you feel. Please.' He slid his hand around to cup the side of her face, its warmth a comfort that she'd missed.

Her first instinct was to pull away and run, but the

sad expression in his eyes beseeched her to stand and deliver.

'I've already tried and you didn't listen. Why is it different now?'

He wiped away the tears that spilled down her cheeks in slow rivulets before hauling her into his arms and burying his face in her hair. 'Please don't cry. I can't bear it. I'm so sorry for hurting you.'

She stiffened at the first contact of hard chest wall but soon relaxed into him, melding against his body as if she was made for it. And the last of her resistance melted away as he held her close and whispered into her ear, 'I love you so much. You're my world, my everything. I know I don't deserve it but please hear me out.'

She snuggled into him as her tears subsided, too drained to reply. His masculine scent filled her nostrils, calling to her receptors on a deeper level, beckoning her to fill herself with this man in every way.

His words filled her with a hope that begged to give him a chance.

Leaning back slightly, she looked up. 'What happened with us? What went wrong?'

The sadness she glimpsed in his eyes made her want to hold on to him for ever. 'A combination of things, starting with a major hang-up I've had about my mother for most of my life.'

Oh, great. He was a mummy's boy?

'Though I'll never forgive her for running out on

my dad and breaking his heart, I recently learned a few truths that set the record straight.'

Her hand flew to her mouth. 'Your father! How is he?'

'He's fine. In fact, I owe him a lot for making me see sense. For a psychologist who prides himself on reading people, I really botched up with you, didn't I?'

She shrugged and smiled for the first time since Friday night. 'Hey, I've already told you what I think of your counselling skills. On national radio too!'

He laughed and scooped her closer. 'And my ego hasn't recovered since.' His smile faded as he tucked a strand of hair behind her ear. 'You must've gone through hell growing up. I'm sorry for dismissing it the other night.'

'You don't know the half of it,' she said, understanding she would have to tell him everything for a fresh start.

As she opened her mouth to speak, he held a finger up to her lips. 'You don't have to tell me if you don't want to. I trust you, and it took the fact that I almost lost you to wake me up to it.'

She kissed his finger before pushing it away. 'I need to do this for me.'

'Okay, but why don't we sit down?' His eyes lit up as he placed a hand on her belly. 'After all, you're carrying precious cargo in there.'

At the possessive look of love on his face, her

heart slammed against her ribs. This man loved her and their baby. What more could she ask for?

Sure, he owed her an explanation for the rotten way he'd treated her, but how could she blame him when she had enough hang-ups to keep him occupied till their fiftieth anniversary?

He led her into a sunny family room adjacent to the kitchen, where she glimpsed champagne chilling in a bucket next to two flutes.

She quirked an eyebrow and looked at him. 'Cocky, weren't you?'

'Hopeful, not cocky. There's a difference.'

He made a move to uncork the bottle before glancing back at her uncertainly.

'Water will be fine.'

'Cheap date,' he muttered as he filled two glasses from the tap and added a slice of lemon to each.

'But you love me anyway,' she said, sending him a coy smile as he handed it to her.

'Now who's cocky?' He sat next to her on the couch, his hand resting on her knee, sending heat streaking through her body. 'Where were we?'

Rather than her hunger for him abating with the enforced absence of the last few days, it had grown to monstrous proportions and it took all her willpower not to jump him.

'We're discussing how screwed up we both are. Shall you go first or shall I?'

He tilted his glass towards her and smiled. 'Ladies first.'

'Okay.' She settled back on the couch, wishing they'd done this weeks ago. If so, it would've saved her a lot of stress—and a fortune in doughnuts and tissues. 'You know about my weight problem, right? The part I didn't tell you was that I became so obsessed about losing weight that I went the other way, losing so much I collapsed.'

His grip tightened on her leg. 'Were you anorexic?'

She shook her head. 'No, thank goodness, but almost. When I collapsed, I spent some time in hospital, and that was enough to get me back on track. I absolutely hated the place and would've done anything to get out so I started eating and actually began to feel good about myself. However, the medical team told me something that changed my life.'

She closed her eyes, wondering how many times she'd relived that fateful moment over the years and wishing she could find that doctor right now and shove her pregnancy test in his face.

Taking a deep breath, she opened her eyes. Lachlan hadn't moved a muscle—he didn't push her or demand to know the truth. Instead, he waited patiently.

'They told me I'd probably never have children.'

'*What?*' he exploded, his anger surprising her.

'I suppose they thought it was true at the time. However, it changed my life. At least how I related to men,' she rushed on, before she lost her confidence to tell him everything. 'Most men want a child to prove their potency to the world and that's the one thing I thought I couldn't give them. The first guy I really fell for did a runner when I told him the truth, despite vowing to love me for ever, so I picked up the pieces of my fragile self-esteem again, and moved on. The second—well, he was just as bad. I've only dated casually since, for that very reason. However, when you came along…' She shrugged and covered his hand with hers. 'Despite my intentions to hold you at bay, I fell for you.'

He clicked his fingers in a lightbulb moment. 'That's why you backed off from me, isn't it? That day I came to your office I prattled on how about how much having a large family meant to me. And you thought you couldn't give me that?'

She nodded and he hauled her into his arms.

'You put my feelings ahead of your own?' He stroked her hair, a soothing gesture she would never tire of. 'You're a remarkable woman, Keely Rhodes. Our child is going to have one very special mother.'

She wriggled out of his embrace. 'Hang on a minute, buster. That's me off the hook. How about you?'

'Like I said, my mother left me with enough emotional baggage to weigh down a jet plane. She lied, cheated and generally devastated my father before walking out on us. Hence my obsession with honesty.'

'Go on.' She watched a myriad emotions flicker across his face, knowing how painful this must be for him but needing to hear it anyway.

'When you were holding out on me these last few weeks, I was going out of my mind. If you couldn't tell me about that phone call, I wondered what else you were hiding. Add to that your walk-out at the café, plus the way you kept clamming up or over-reacting over what I thought were innocent comments, and I was ready to throttle you. Then Chrystal mentioned something about you and some guy Aidan the other night and I lost it.'

'I'll kill her,' she muttered under her breath. 'Aidan is this loser who pops into Accounts on occasion. I thought he'd be perfect for my assistant, Lucy, which turned out to be false anyway. Why would Chrystal start a rumour—?'

She burst out laughing and refrained from slapping her head to knock some sense into herself. 'You're her next victim and she wanted me off the scene! Why, the little scheming tramp. And you believed her?'

He had the grace to look sheepish. 'In all honesty, I was probably looking for an excuse to have it out with you, so I latched on to her words and they fuelled my own insecurities. Your jealousy act set me off; that's what I thought you were doing, acting. When I heard about this other guy it reminded me of my mother, and when you flung that bit about a possible baby at me…she'd done the same thing to my dad. Or so I'd thought. Dad set me straight and made me see what a mess I was making of my own life, blaming you when you're nothing like her.'

She could strangle Chrystal with her bare hands, but in a way she owed her. If she hadn't interfered, Keely might've danced around her past for months yet, driving a bigger wedge between them, and Lachlan wouldn't have discovered the truth about his mother.

'You said you loved me; my mother never loved my father.' He rubbed a hand over his face, as if trying to erase the past. 'I was so ashamed for flinging your declaration back in your face that I stayed away on the weekend, trying to concoct a scheme to win you back.'

'And this is it?'

He grinned, the warmth of his smile sending her pulse racing. 'Partially. Lucy helped get you here and I hoped the truth would do the rest.'

'You're getting there. Keep going.'

Lucy would have a lot of explaining to do tomorrow. Though how could she fault her assistant for bringing the man she loved back into her life? She should give her a rise rather than a scolding.

'What do you think of this house?'

His question came from left field, though nothing should surprise her in this all-round weird week. Over the last seven days she'd discovered she was pregnant, been dumped and then reunited with the love of her life, and, if the rumours were correct, gained that promotion she'd been hankering for.

Raquel had scheduled a meeting with her for the end of the week, and she hoped the Director of

Graphic Design position would be hers. She'd done a damn good job with the Brant assignment, even if she had taken the shadowing bit to extremes! Though how the Rottie would react when she learned she'd lose a second director to motherhood didn't bear thinking about.

She glanced around the room, admiring the airy open plan with afternoon light spilling in from the floor-to-ceiling windows, the comfortable furniture, the mix of modern with eclectic.

'I love it from what I've seen of it. My apartment is the antithesis of it, but this place feels welcoming, like a real home.'

The corners of his mouth twitched. 'Good, I'm glad you like it. I bought it weeks ago, with us in mind. Think you could live here?'

'Huh?' The idea that he'd had so much faith in their relationship made her feel guilty all over again for holding him at bay.

'I'm the new owner, and I'd hoped my future wife would love it as much as I do.'

Her mouth dropped open and his soft chuckles echoed in the silence as he cupped her chin and gently closed it.

'That's right, Keely. I'm asking you to marry me.' He kissed her, a slow, lingering kiss that lit a fire deep within. 'I love you, and would be honoured if you'd agree to be my wife.'

'I love you too,' she whispered, her heart tripping with the extent of how much, 'and the answer is yes.

Though I don't know if I can live with a man who isn't perfect.'

He closed the short distance between them by pulling her on to his lap. 'In that case, you'd better concentrate on the bits that are perfect.'

He lowered his lips to hers. 'Starting with this.'

# EPILOGUE

*'Note to self: ditch* Keely's Collection. *Perfect
man found—and he's amazing.'*
Keely, new convert to the 'happily-ever-after'
philosophy.

KEELY strolled into the conference room, using every
ounce of self-control not to do a happy dance and
blurt out the truth as soon as she saw her friends.

'Hey, how are you, sweetie?' Emma joined her at
the coffee machine and refilled her cup. 'Over that
bug yet? Feeling okay about everything else?'

Keely nodded and smiled, resisting the urge to
blab to the world that she wasn't just feeling okay,
she was feeling downright amazing. The love of a
good man, a marriage proposal and an unexpected
baby on the way would do that to a woman.

'I'm fine. Though I have got some news for you.'
She bit back a grin at the anticipated reaction from
her romantic friend. Not just the fact that she'd reunited with Lachlan but they were starting a family
to boot.

She'd omitted that pertinent fact when crying on
the girls' shoulders over the weekend—she hadn't
wanted them to rush over to Lachlan and do some-

180

thing crazy—like dragging him back to her handcuffed and forcing him to marry her. Though now that she came to think about it…it would've speeded up the whole process and saved her days of heartbreaking misery.

Tahlia walked into the room at that moment and headed over to join them. 'I hope it's got nothing to do with that louse Lachlan. Good riddance to bad rubbish, no matter how gorgeous.'

Keely filled her mug with hot water and camomile tea, knowing her caffeine withdrawal was going to be hell but willing to do anything for the precious life inside her. 'Actually, it has got something to do with him.'

Tahlia's eyes narrowed as her gaze swept from Keely's tea up to her face. 'What's going on? I thought he was history? And why are you drinking *that*?'

Keely sipped at the tea and tried not to grimace, failing miserably. Maybe she'd try peppermint or raspberry tomorrow.

'You're pregnant, aren't you?' Emma blurted out, her eyes twinkling with barely suppressed excitement.

Keely's eyebrows shot up. 'How did you know?'

Emma let out a whoop and smothered her in a ferocious hug while Tahlia gaped in open-mouthed amazement before muttering, 'I need to sit down.'

Laughing at her friends' reactions, she disengaged

from Emma's arms and gestured at the table. 'Why don't we all have a seat and I'll explain everything?'

'Good idea,' Tahlia said, shaking her head and looking totally perplexed while Emma grinned as if she'd just won the Lottery. 'I take it you're happy about the news, despite the louse's defection?'

Keely filled a glass with water, deciding to ditch the herbal tea for now. It would have to grow on her, as everything else about her would grow in the next few months.

'I'm ecstatic,' she said, hugging a protective arm around her middle. 'Oh, and I'd prefer it if you'd stop calling my future husband a louse.'

This time Emma joined Tahlia in the open-mouth stakes, before screeching, 'You're getting *married*?'

'Yeah. It's great, isn't it?'

Emma let out an excited squeal and clapped her hands together. 'This is fantastic! How romantic. When did all this happen?'

'On one of those dirty weekends away, I'd imagine,' Tahlia said, sending Keely a wicked smile.

Emma waved away Tahlia's comment. 'Not that part. Last thing we knew, you were sobbing all over us, telling us what a jerk he'd been in dumping you. And now you're getting married?'

'I was kind of premature about the jerk bit. He's still pretty perfect.'

'The marriage isn't just about the baby, is it?' A slight frown marred Tahlia's brow, her ever-practical and blunt assessment of the situation leaving Keely in no doubt as to how much her friend actually cared.

'Uh-uh. He'd already said he loved me before he knew about the baby. And he'd bought us a house to prove it.' She patted her belly and smiled. 'I guess this little person will just hurry along our wedding plans, that's all.'

Emma sat bolt upright and rubbed her hands together. 'Fabulous. We've got a wedding to plan.'

'And a baby shower,' Tahlia added, leaning over and hugging Keely tightly.

Keely laughed and blinked back tears. She could blame her swinging emotions on hormones, but she'd rather attribute the sudden waterworks to her best friends and their unswerving loyalty.

For someone who'd been alone and floundering for so many years, she wanted to pinch herself now to see if all this was real—great job, wonderful friends, and now the perfect man and their precious miracle.

'Thanks, you guys. For everything.' She dabbed at her eyes, thankful for waterproof mascara, and pointed at the files on the table. 'Now, we'd better get stuck into work before the Rottie gets stuck into us. Any other goss from you before we get started?'

Emma's eyes glowed briefly before she opened the file in front of her and started shuffling papers. 'Harry's coming to town for his yearly visit soon, so I'm kind of looking forward to that.'

Tahlia hooted. 'Kind of? Bet you can't think of

anything else, you're so obsessed with the guy.' She paused and winked at Keely. 'Though I reckon he's a figment of your imagination. We've never seen him in the flesh, so to speak.'

'And you won't, with that attitude,' Emma said, blushing furiously.

Still caught up in her own love fest, Keely understood exactly where Emma was coming from. If she loved the guy, she should go for it. After all, look where that philosophy had got her.

'We'd really like to meet him, hon. And if he's as special as you say he is why don't you throw caution to the wind and tell the guy how you feel?'

'Yeah, why don't you jump his bones already?' Tahlia chimed in, a smirk on her face.

'I'll think about it,' Emma muttered, her blush deepening.

Tahlia shrugged and reached for her file. 'If you don't do it, we will.'

'You wouldn't dare!'

'Just try me,' Tahlia said, patting Emma's cheek before settling back in her seat. 'No goss from me, so let's get to work.'

Keely chuckled, loving the familiar banter and knowing she was going to miss it while away on maternity leave. Though she knew the girls would be visiting on a regular basis, it wouldn't be the same as their D&Ms in the conference room. Not that she'd have time to worry about it; her little bundle of joy would be monopolising all her time as she discovered what motherhood was all about.

'Here's the finished product for *Flirt*,' she said, handing copies to Emma and Tahlia.

However, before they could take a look, Lucy stuck her head around the door. 'Sorry to interrupt, ladies, but you have a client waiting in your office, Keely. I told him you were busy, but he said it would only take a minute and he wouldn't take no for an answer.'

Keely bit the inside of her cheek to stop herself from laughing as she noticed Lucy's wink and 'come here' hand gesture, which could only mean one thing.

Her *client* needed some immediate attention, and she was more than ready to give it to him.

'Back in five, girls,' she said, casually strolling to the door when in fact she wanted to pick up her feet and fly to her office.

However, she forced herself to walk sedately down the corridor, her anticipation mounting with every step. It had only been a few hours since she'd kissed her new fiancé goodbye, but one could never have too many kisses from a man like Lachlan.

Reaching her door, she schooled her face into a professional mask with effort and entered the room. 'I hear you have some important business to discuss. What can I do for you?'

Lachlan spun round from the window and crossed the room in two seconds flat, hauling her into his arms so quickly that all the breath rushed out of her.

Not that she minded; she was getting used to feeling breathless around him.

'You can start by wrapping up whatever you're in the middle of and coming to lunch with me.' His hands played in a leisurely way along her spine, sending electrifying tingles shooting every which way.

'I have work to do.' She tried a mock frown and failed dismally.

He ran a finger slowly down her cheek, letting it rest against her bottom lip, which practically quivered under his touch. 'How about you *work* on me?'

She shook her head and chuckled. 'Doc, you're crazy.'

His lips brushed hers in a sweet, lingering kiss, the kind that she could get used to for the rest of her life. 'Crazy in love with you.'

If you enjoyed what you just read,
then we've got an offer you can't resist!

# Take 2 bestselling love stories FREE!

# Plus get a FREE surprise gift!

**Clip this page and mail it to Harlequin Reader Service®**

| IN U.S.A. | IN CANADA |
|---|---|
| 3010 Walden Ave. | P.O. Box 609 |
| P.O. Box 1867 | Fort Erie, Ontario |
| Buffalo, N.Y. 14240-1867 | L2A 5X3 |

**YES!** Please send me 2 free Harlequin Romance® novels and my free surprise gift. After receiving them, if I don't wish to receive anymore, I can return the shipping statement marked cancel. If I don't cancel, I will receive 6 brand-new novels every month, before they're available in stores! In the U.S.A., bill me at the bargain price of $3.57 plus 25¢ shipping & handling per book and applicable sales tax, if any*. In Canada, bill me at the bargain price of $4.05 plus 25¢ shipping & handling per book and applicable taxes**. That's the complete price and a savings of 10% off the cover prices—what a great deal! I understand that accepting the 2 free books and gift places me under no obligation ever to buy any books. I can always return a shipment and cancel at any time. Even if I never buy another book from Harlequin, the 2 free books and gift are mine to keep forever.

186 HDN DZ72
386 HDN DZ73

| Name | (PLEASE PRINT) | |
|---|---|---|
| Address | Apt.# | |
| City | State/Prov. | Zip/Postal Code |

*Not valid to current Harlequin Romance® subscribers.*
*Want to try another series? Call 1-800-873-8635*
*or visit www.morefreebooks.com.*

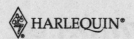

**HARLEQUIN®**

━━━━━━━━━━━━━━━━━━━━━━━━━━━━━━━━━━

# H A R L E Q U I N   R O M A N C E®

━━━━━━━━━━━━━━━━━━━━━━━━━━━━━━━━━━

## Coming Next Month

### #3867 THEIR NEW-FOUND FAMILY Rebecca Winters

As a single mom, Rachel Marsden has always tried to do her best
by her daughter. So when Natalie's long-lost father, Tris Monbrisson,
shows up Rachel swallows her feelings. For the summer they will
move to Tris's beautiful home in the mountains of Switzerland. But as
she and Tris fall into the role of mother and father, the secrets of the
past unravel....

### #3868 STRICTLY BUSINESS Liz Fielding and Hannah Bernard (2 stories in 1 volume)

*The Temp and the Tycoon* by Liz Fielding—Her new boss,
Jude Radcliff, is all work and no play...can Tallie persuade him to
live life to the max—with her...?

*The Fiancé Deal* by Hannah Bernard—Louise Henderson is
fighting for the same promotion as sexy lawyer David Tyler. She
needs a fiancé fast—and David's the best man for the job!

### #3869 MISTLETOE MARRIAGE Jessica Hart

For Sophie Beckwith, this Christmas means facing the ex who
dumped her and then married her sister! Only one person can help:
her best friend Bram. Bram used to be engaged to Sophie's sister,
and now, determined to show the lovebirds that they've moved on,
he's come up with a plan: he's proposed to Sophie!

### #3870 THE SHOCK ENGAGEMENT by Ally Blake

Emma's colleagues and friends are delighted she is marrying the
gorgeous and successful dot com millionaire Harry Buchanan—but
their engagement is purely for convenience. Harry will get out of
the excruciating "hunkiest male" competition and Emma will save
her job. Only, Emma has dreamed of marrying Harry for years, and
acting engaged is pure torture....

**Office Gossip**

Keely, Emma and Tahlia work together at a small, trendy design company in Melbourne. They've become the best of friends, meeting for breakfast, chatting over a mid-morning coffee and a donut—or going for a cocktail after work. They've loved being single in the city…but now three gorgeous new men are about to enter their work lives, transform their love lives—and give them loads more to gossip about!

Don't miss each story in this great new trilogy brought to you by Harlequin Romance®!

**From sexy bosses to surprise babies—
these ladies have got everyone talking!**

This month, October 2005
*Impossibly Pregnant* by Nicola Marsh, #3866

A positive pregnancy test is a surprise for Keely!

Next month, November 2005:
*The Shock Engagement* by Ally Blake, #3870

Emma has always dreamed of marrying Harry.
Now they're engaged—but it's all a sham.
Will he ever be hers for real…?

The month after that, December 2005:
*Taking on the Boss* by Darcy Maguire, #3874

Tahlia's furious that the promotion she's been working so hard for has been given to someone else!
He's now her new boss—and he's *gorgeous!*

Dear Reader,

I love living in the vibrant city of Melbourne. The cosmopolitan cafés, the fabulous shopping and best of all, bookstores galore!

Keely Rhodes, the sassy Web site designer in *Impossibly Pregnant,* alongside her best friends Emma and Tahlia, are city girls who thrive on Melbourne's vibe. Keely works at Southbank on the Yarra River, lives in the beautiful bayside suburb of Port Melbourne and has her hands full with her gorgeous leading man, Lachlan Brant.

While Lachlan prefers surfing at Torquay and unwinding at Hepburn Springs, two towns not far from Melbourne, the city has its own charm, starting with the woman who turns his world upside down!

Writing Keely's story has been rewarding and I hope you get a taste of what magical Melbourne has to offer. Ally Blake and Darcy Maguire continue the fun in their linked books for the OFFICE GOSSIP series. I hope you enjoy the stories as much as we did creating them.

Happy reading,

**Nicola**

www.nicolamarsh.com